****

Through Rose's Colored Glasses

A Secondhand Homicide Whodunit

Book 1

Myrl V. Williams

Back Porch Literature

****

Myrl V. Williams

Help support Colorado Springs businesses

Rosco's Coffee House

www.Roscoscoffeehouse.com

Flying W Ranch & Chuckwagon

www.FlyingW.com

In loving memory of my dear friend, Jim Gaines.

Thank you to my son, Storm, for all his help and support.

Thank you to Davon, for great inspiration.

Thank you to my family and all my friends who have been

encouraging and supportive through this journey.

1

Up until that moment, I had had impeccable balance. I mean, I had been a gymnast all through school (though not the Olympic athlete I'd envisioned myself to be, Mary Lou Retton, I was not), and I had practiced martial arts once upon a time, achieving two belt levels. Despite all of this, the next step I took was going to change my life forever; in ways that I could not even begin to imagine. Well, at least that's what I'm going to blame it on, because I don't remember anything being different until after that moment.

Colorado winters can be brutal and bitterly cold, especially for a 50+ year old woman returning to the work force, after being a stay-at-home wife and mother for the last 20 years. My foot hit the patch of black ice and sent me rocking and reeling. I can only imagine how ridiculous

I appeared, arms flailing wildly, like a windmill out of control on a blustery Kansas afternoon.

Poor Peyton (my adorable little shih tzu) was jerked from his feet with a loud yelp, as I went ass over tea kettle. and landed with a bone-jarring thud upon the snow-covered pavement. The back of my head slammed into the ground, worthy of any Von Miller sack. Red and black numbers flashed in my mind like a spinning roulette wheel, my eyeball the bouncing white marble. Eighteen red! And then the colorless ball jumped to black, as did my consciousness.

I'm not exactly sure how long I was lying there on the cold, hard ground, but Peyton's sandpaper tongue, licking my cheek, eventually brought me around. I blinked rapidly as a brilliant array of phosphenes danced in my field of vision. The gray sky above me swirled violently out of control. Woozy and struggling to sit up, I checked to make sure Peyton hadn't used me as his own personal fire hydrant, while I was out in lala land. Thank goodness, there were no wet, yellow marks around me. Luckily, his leash still wrapped around my wrist, saved me from having to chase after my mangy little mutt.

I crawled over to the white laden lawn to stand, snow and gravel digging into my palms; I certainly didn't need a repeat performance of my wayward acrobatics. I was grateful none of the neighborhood hooligans were out this early to make fun of me and my antics. A quick check to make sure my baby, Peyton, wasn't injured and I headed home, overly careful with each and every step now.

In the distance, up the hill, I could see the gray two-story monstrosity in which I lived. The complex consisted of several ugly stucco buildings which hadn't been painted in several eons. Giving Peyton's leash a slight tug, we ambled gingerly towards 'Alcatraz', my not so affectionate nickname for the dingy gray structures.

As I made my way up the steps to my apartment, I tenderly rubbed the goose egg which was beginning to bloom on the back of my head. I could, with complete confidence, predict a raging headache would shortly ensue. Voices from my childhood flitted around in my head, "Don't fall asleep or you'll slip into a coma" and "You need to see a doctor, to make sure you haven't sustained a concussion".

An ER visit was out of the question, beside the fact I didn't have the time, I also didn't have the money or insurance for that costly venture. I had a business to run, I needed to get down to my shop and open the doors for all the enthusiastic purveyors of vintage and antique treasures. So, the headache building in my now frazzled brain would have to wait, at least for the time being.

Fumbling with the keys, in my now frozen and numb fingers (I'd forgotten my gloves on the kitchen counter), I unlocked the door, then slamming it shut, trudged straight down the hall towards the bathroom.

The steaming water of the shower served multiple purposes. I hated the cold, so this was the quickest way to warm myself and the moist heat would do wonders for the ache throbbing in my neck. It would also ensure a pleasant reboot to my morning. Wiping away the steam from the mirror, I tried to examine the back of my head, unfortunately with no success. At least there hadn't been any blood, I rationalized, still ignoring those voices from my childhood.

One hot shower and couple of aspirin later, I was dressed and ready to get my day moving in a different direction. I buttered two slices of sourdough toast, threw on a couple of slices of avocado, and grabbed my beverage of choice, an ice cold 20-ounce Coke. *This* was the breakfast of champions.

After feeding Peyton and giving him a treat, for his unwitting participation in my botched circus act, I turned on his favorite show, 'Scooby Doo', and headed out for work, telling him to behave while I was gone. He glanced at me briefly before turning back to the talking dog on the television screen.

"Love you, too," I told him, shaking my head, and closing the door behind me.

The Back Porch on Bijou was mine and my business partner's ambitious undertaking. It was a cozy shop on the west side of town, which dealt in antique, vintage, and classic 'junk', for the lack of a better word and one my ex used to describe my passion. He and my son, Hub, would bemoan the times I asked them to move my 'stuff' from one corner of the garage to another, asking why I would want to keep all this old crap, yet move it none-the-less. Cause, if momma ain't happy, ain't nobody happy.

Thank goodness I hadn't let them dissuade me. That old 'junk' (as they liked to call it) had been the cornerstone of my inventory. All those trips to secondhand stores, thrift and consignment shops were going to pay off, hopefully in a big way. Who knew the latest trend would be people furnishing their homes with thrift store finds, estate sale trinkets and repurposed furniture? I got a great deal of satisfaction from taking an old piece and giving it new life. It brought me immense joy seeing a customer's eyes light up when they found that perfect item.

I wandered the musty isles of my favorite secondhand shop, Thrifty Rags, an old red brick building on the west side, in Old Colorado City. This morning I was making the rounds of several different thrift stores, my weekly circuit through Colorado Springs. I was searching for old pieces of glass, dinner, and silverware, along with any other gem that caught my eye.

And, what caught my eye this morning: a pair of vintage, pink cat-eye glasses adorned with a plethora of glittering rhinestones. Come to mama!

Picking up the delicate glasses and holding them up to the light, I examined the lenses for any scratches and the frames for any cracks, finding neither. I slipped them on and checked out my appearance in a nearby tabletop mirror. Or what I perceived to be a mirror, because what I saw was an elderly woman staring back at me through the glass.

I blinked.

I took the glasses off and stared at my bewildered reflection. Yes, it was indeed a mirror. I picked it up, examined the back side of it and didn't notice anything odd.

What the heck?

Turning the spectacles over in my hand I examined them again, trying to determine if something may have been hologramed onto the lens or embedded within. Nothing.

I glanced around the store, to make sure I wasn't being filmed for some crazy reality show that punks people. Noticing nothing of the sort and spying no hidden cameras or reality TV hosts, I put them back on and observed the same elderly woman peeking back at me through the salmon pink frames.

I blinked again. She blinked in unison with me, her blue eyes shining brightly, however as *my* mouth fell open, hers curled up into a cute, knowing smile, accentuating the fine wrinkles at the corners of her eyes and mouth.

What the fudge?

Pulling the glasses off, I threw them to the counter in a mild panic and stared wide eyed at the possessed frames. I considered brandishing a crucifix in their direction, positive they'd burst into flames if I did. But Gretchen, the store owner and a dear friend of my mother's, would be none too happy if I burnt her shop to the ground, so I quickly nixed the idea.

Do do, do do, do do, do do; the theme song from The Twilight Zone echoed in my head.

What in the heck was going on? That crack to the head, I'd suffered this morning, must have been worse than I thought. Maybe I *should* make a trip to the hospital, or at least call my doctor.

Another passing patron snatched up the glasses and tried them on, gazing into the same mirror which I had. I watched her carefully from the corner of my eye, observing her behavior for any kind of reaction. She tilted her noggin from side to side, before shaking her head and putting them back. Evidently, she wasn't seeing the same freakish things I was.

Taking them in hand, I stalled for several minutes before I whisked them to the register and purchased them, along with all my other buys of the morning, curiosity winning out over my fear. I was becoming increasingly interested to know who this cute, little old lady was and why she seemed to be appearing only to me.

"Did you find anything for the shop?" Gretchen asked, while she rang up my purchases.

"A few and then some," I replied, my brain trying to process my strange occurrence. "Thanks, Gretch. I'll see you next week."

"Give your mother my love."

"I will," I promised, waving as I left the shop.

In somewhat of a daze, I made it to the car. I put the bag on the front passenger seat and just stared at it, wondering what in the heck had happened inside the store. After a good ten minutes, I pulled the glasses out and tried them on again. As I peered into my rearview mirror, there she was. The sweet face of the older woman stared back at me, gently rocking back and forth, and humming an unfamiliar tune.

What in the hell was happening to me?

My hands trembled as I put the frames back in the crinkled tissue paper, which Gretchen had so kindly wrapped them in. I headed down to the shop, utterly perplexed and completely curious. No longer interested in continuing my shopping circuit for the day.

The fifteen-minute drive down to the shop was filled with puzzlement and awe. I kept glancing over at the bag on the passenger's seat, finding what I was experiencing, incredibly hard to believe. There *must* be some kind of logical explanation. There had to be, because this was defying all rationale.

Was this real or was it the whack to my head this morning? I promised myself I would call Dr. V. as soon as I got to the shop.

The Back Porch on Bijou is a small two-story, stucco building, which at one time served as the neighborhood grocery store for the west side. To make us stand out, we had painted it a tasteful, robin's egg blue. The yellow awnings, we installed over the two lower windows, highlighted the brilliant sunflowers we planted each spring in the flower boxes beneath the windows. White shutters flanked each of the windows on every side of the colorful structure.

Inside, it was packed with shelf upon shelf of all the inventory which Helen and I had acquired over the years, in our endeavor to supply the locals with vintage and classic gems. Tasteful vignettes created enticing displays, inviting customers to envision an entire look rather than just a single piece within their own space. There was always a pleasant seasonal scent permeating the interior, to welcome our guests. While classic Rock and Roll from the 50's, 60's and 70's added to our ambiance.

Helen, my business partner, hadn't arrived yet, so the store was dark and quiet, making it the perfect time to explore the strange glasses some more. All the other purchases I'd made, I put into the storeroom so I could research and price later. The glasses, however, accompanied me to my desk. It was quite a while before I made my decision. Exhaling slowly and with trembling hands, I tentatively brought them to my face.

As I took in what was happening, I found myself sitting in a rocking chair, surrounded by several cats and a pile of knitting in my lap. I could feel the yarn's softness beneath my fingertips. The smell of cat pee assaulted my nostrils, and I wrinkled my nose at the offensive odor. From where I sat rocking, I counted seven of the furry, sniffle generating beasts, just lazing around. The gentle tick-tock of a clock thrummed in the background with a mild, lulling beat.

As the tiny bird in the clock cuckooed twice, I gazed down at the watch on my wrist, except this wasn't 'my' wrist. This wrist, and the hand attached, were deeply wrinkled, and covered with several brown age spots.

"Two o'clock," I voiced aloud, "almost time for tea with Ethel."

Who in the hell was Ethel?

I shook my head, trying to clear it, trying to comprehend what was going on.

Getting up and walking into a quaint kitchen, painted a soft, buttercream yellow and decorated with roosters and hens, I began filling a whistling teapot with water from the tap. The stainless-steel kettle slipped from my grasp and clattered to the floor, as I felt pain piercing two spots within my back. My hands gripped the countertop and I fell to my knees before slipping face down onto the cool tile floor. As the world began to fade to gray, I saw a pair of high heels standing next to me.

I pulled the glasses off, my heart beating wildly out of control. When I opened my eyes, my head was cocked to the side and I was squinting to see who was wearing the shoes. Oh, did I mention… I was also laying on the floor of the shop.

"What in the world are you doing down there?" Helen asked, hovering over me, lights now glaring into my eyes. Obviously, I hadn't heard her enter.

"I think I just witnessed a murder," I answered, dumbstruck.

"What? Where?"

Helen's head jerked around the room searching for some clue as to what I was babbling about.

"You're going to think I'm crazy…" I paused.

"Well, lucky for you, I already think you're crazy," she asserted, offering me a hand. "I mean look at you, passed out on the floor with those ridiculous glasses on. Where in the world did you get those hideous things?"

"I wasn't passed out," I answered, struggling to get my out-of-shape carcass to my knees. "I told you, I was witnessing a murder."

She helped me to my feet and raised her eyebrows. "A murder? Do tell."

"Every time I put these glasses on," I waved them in front of her, "I become the old lady who was wearing them when she died. Or at least I think she died."

A concerned expression pained her face and she reached out to feel my forehead.

"Did you bang your head or something?"

"As a matter of fact, I did. However, 'that' is beside the point."

I still had a dull ache at the back of my head and my neck was now stiff and tight. In any case, I couldn't deal with that distraction right now.

"Give me those," Helen said, taking the glasses from me and putting them on. "What am I supposed to be seeing? Because I see nothing but this room and your crazy self."

She thrust them back at me.

I took them in hand and tried to explain. "I become the lady who owned them. I was rocking in her rocking chair, knitting something in my lap and had a dozen or so cats staring at me. When I got up to make tea for Ethel, someone stabbed me in the back."

"Ethel? Who *is* Ethel?"

"That is what I'd like to know," I wondered, pointing my finger at her. "I don't think she is the murderer, though. Ethel is a classic name and the woman I saw had on red high heels. I don't think an old lady could handle heels that spikey or that color."

"You saw the murderer?" Helen asked in disbelief.

"Only her shoes. I was on the floor dying, remember?"

"I can't believe I'm having this discussion with you," she held her hand up and rolled her eyes. "Did you go get yourself checked for a concussion?"

"No."

"Well, maybe you ought to. You need to pick up the phone and call your doctor. You know, the really attractive one. Isn't he single?"

"No, he is not."

Helen gave me a halfhearted shrug and turned to her computer.

I sat at my desk and tossed the frames down next to my keyboard. Picking up my phone, I pulled Dr. V's number up. Debating the idea, I chose not to hit send, eventually swiping the potential call away. I tapped my fingers several times on my desk before I picked up the glasses and put them back on.

Reliving the scene to where I was lying on the floor, through a gray haze, I heard a woman's voice bitterly say, "Rest in peace, Rose."

I peeled the glasses off again.

"Her name was Rose," I shouted excitedly. "The lady who died was named Rose."

Helen began typing furiously on her keyboard, with a random clickity clack of her nails on the keys.

"Marlie, come over here and look at this," she urged, frantically waving me over.

Leaning over her shoulder, I peered at the article she had pulled up on the monitor: Local Retirement Village Resident Killed in Apparent Robbery. Scanning the article from six months earlier, I saw the name of the victim: Rose O'Brien. She had been stabbed in the back with her own knitting needles, during an apparent robbery. Her long-time friend, Ethel McDonald, had been the one to discover the body and was quoted as saying 'She was just lying there with her size 13 knitting needles sticking out of her back'. The home had also been ransacked in a possible burglary. There were no signs of forced entry.

23

Rose O'Brien's plump cheeks, and face, framed by her silky, snow-white hair, peered out from the photo attached to the clip. The same intense blue eyes now stared back at me from the computer screen. *This* was the woman I had seen in the mirror down at Thrifty Rags and again in my rearview mirror.

"That's her!" I shouted, pointing at the screen. "That's the woman I keep seeing."

Helen and I stood with our mouths open, staring at one another in disbelief.

"Oh, my gawd," we marveled, simultaneously.

"I remembered thinking when this happened how weird it was, that she was stabbed with her knitting needles. I mean who does that, and to an old lady, none the less. It was her name that jogged my memory because I've always loved the name Rose," Helen explained. "I almost named Christina, Rose."

"That explains why I felt pain in two spots on my back," realizing it was the knitting needles I'd felt.

"Wait, you felt her getting stabbed? Did it hurt?" Helen asked concerned, lifting the back of my shirt, looking for any visible puncture wounds.

Thinking back to my vision, I didn't actually feel pain when I, or when Rose, was stabbed. It was more of a pressure and realizing she'd been stabbed.

I shook my head, "Not real pain, more of a sensation."

"Maybe her ghost is attached to the glasses?" Helen suggested.

I shook my head again.

"Another woman down at Thrifty Rags tried them on and didn't seem to have detected Rose's presence. And you tried them on too," I pointed out.

Helen screwed up her face. "Hmmm, I wonder why only you are seeing and feeling her?"

"Was her murder ever solved? And why don't I remember this?"

"I think it was last October when you were down in Nashville, visiting your sister. I don't remember seeing anything about it being solved."

Helen did another internet search and found it had not, to date, been solved. The police department was asking anyone with information regarding the case to contact them.

"You need to call the detective in charge of the case," Helen urged.

"And tell him what, exactly? That I experienced Rose's death because I *happened* to stumble upon a pair of her glasses in a thrift store and they showed me her murder?" I rambled, laughing at the absurdity of the thought.

"It does sound a bit crazy, when you say it like *that*." I couldn't miss the hint of sarcasm in her tone.

"Only a bit."

Neither of us said anything for several minutes.

"So, what are you going to do?" Helen finally broke the silence.

"I don't think I'd have anything to add to the investigation. I'm sure the police know everything and more, than I do," I reasoned.

"What if they don't? What if they don't know about the woman in the heels?"

This was indeed a possibility, since the article had also mentioned an apparent burglary, but no mention of a perpetrator.

"I couldn't tell them who she is or give them any kind of description of her. I only saw her shoes."

"What if they're not even looking for a woman, then you *would* have information in reference to the case," she contended.

Sometimes, her logic can be so annoying.

It definitely gave me something to think about the rest of the afternoon, while I was working on pricing our new inventory. In the car, on the way home, I rehearsed what I could possibly say to the lead detective. Everything pouring out of my mouth sounded ludicrous and comical.

I was also trying to wrap my head around this newfound ability I had suddenly acquired. *Was this a permanent condition or a one-time fluke?* I inwardly prayed for the one-time fluke.

2

My cell phone buzzed offensively on the nightstand, waking me from a restful slumber and one steamy, hot dream. Squinting through one eye, I saw that it was Helen, and it was only 5:38 in the morning. Grrrrrr.

"Woman, do you have any idea what time it is?" I grumbled.

"I understand, it's early. Have you seen the paper?" She asked excitedly.

"The paper? No, I was pleasantly observing the inside of my eyelids, thank-you very much. I want you to know, you interrupted an extremely erotic dream," I lectured, hoping to shame her.

It had no effect, whatsoever.

She continued, "There's a lead in the case."

"A lead in what case?" I asked groggily through a yawn, wanting to close my eyes and return to my sensual imagery. A dream that hot doesn't occur every night, you know.

"Your case… Rose's case."

Boom! She had my attention. I sat up and listened, turning on the lamp at my bedside.

"They're trying to locate one of the maintenance men. He retired shortly after the murder and he has just disappeared. No one has seen him in months. It says he is a person of interest. Anyone with information is asked to contact the Colorado Springs Police Department."

"It wasn't a man's feet I saw, and it was a woman's voice who said, 'rest in peace, Rose'."

"It could have been a man in women's shoes," she suggested, "disguising his voice, maybe?"

"The shoes weren't that big. The killer had small feet. I'd say not much larger than mine."

"What if your vision is wrong?"

"It's not *my* vision. It's not as if I conjured this out of thin air," I argued. "It seems to be Rose's final moments projecting themselves through those damn glasses."

29

"I wonder why they picked you? I mean you're not usually a believer in this type of stuff."

"Maybe that's why. They're saying, 'See, you dumbass, there really is mystical, supernatural crap happening out there.' All I know is I busted my head yesterday morning and within an hour, I am living out the death of a murder victim," I grumbled into the phone. "Oh my gawd, do you realize how daft I sound?"

Helen was cackling hysterically on the other end of the conversation. "They always say 'truth is stranger than fiction'."

Truth, I thought, this mystical, ghostly crap was not part of *my* truth. I didn't want anything to do with that kind of nonsense.

Just a brief side note on my friend, Helen. Our small vintage boutique wasn't her first endeavor in entrepreneurship. She had also been part owner in a whimsical, metaphysical bookshop up in Manitou Springs, a few years back. So, she was fully embracing this new quirk in my life. And I imagined she was tickled pink, that I was the recipient of said phenomenon. She believed wholeheartedly in all of this gobbledygook.

"I think you should stop by the police station on your way into the shop today. Maybe the detective will be single and good looking."

"I am *not* interested in single and good looking," I reminded her for the umpteenth time since my divorce.

"Well, maybe he'll be old, fat and bald then," she teased.

"Goodbye," I hung up before she could give me anymore grief about finding a boyfriend.

She means well, I'm just not ready for a relationship yet. Twenty-two years is a long time to be with someone. Plus, there's a whole trust issue lingering there.

Once I was finished with the call, I found Peyton dancing around in the doorway. "Hey, you evil little beast, I'm not ready to get up yet."

He sat and cocked his head as if saying, 'Uh mommy, I have to pee.'

"Ugh, fine," I complained, throwing the blankets off, exposing my flesh to the cool morning temperatures. I stumbled out of bed, cursing Helen, the cold, and my poor dog.

31

Before going out into the winter chill, I kicked the thermostat up to 72 degrees, to ensure a warm cocoon greeted us upon our return. As I said, I detest being cold.

Our short jaunt outside in the brisk morning air, along with the brilliant blue Colorado sky, awakened my senses. The cold burned deep within my lungs, despite this, it was invigorating. Each exhale produced a vaporous cloud of breath, which dissipated within seconds. The smell of wood burning in fireplaces throughout the neighborhood made me long for my old house, rather than the stuffy, confining second-story box I was currently referring to as 'home'.

It's surprising the blows fate will deal you. I had never expected to be living on my own again after being married for twenty-two years, except the ex had different plans. So here I was longing for something I couldn't have (at least for the moment), while trying to figure out how to approach the detective assigned to Rose O'Brien's case with this unbelievable tale.

My fingers drummed rhythmically on the steering wheel as I sat in the parking lot of the Colorado Springs

Police Department (CSPD), debating whether or not I should go inside and try to explain my situation. I jumped, startled by a sharp knock on my window. A clean-cut young man with dark hair, dressed in an off the rack, gray suit, was standing next to my car.

Cautiously, I rolled my window down just a crack.

"Ma'am, you've been sitting here for over thirty minutes. Did you need some help?"

I pursed my lips. "I think I may have information on a case, although I'm not exactly sure."

I squinted; the morning sun was directly behind the man and created a glowing backdrop to his masculine form.

"What kind of case? Burglary? Homicide?"

"Homicide," I responded quickly, nodding my head dumbly, "deffffinitely homicide."

"Well, I'm homicide detective Jace Kendall, maybe I can help."

"Of course, you are," I cringed. Just my luck, the one person I truly didn't want to talk to, would be the one to find me.

Helen would call it a sign.

By the looks of him, he didn't appear old enough to drive, let alone be a homicide detective. I wasn't even sure he was old enough to shave.

"Did you want to come inside and talk about it?" He motioned towards the building.

"I'm not so sure this was a good idea," I floundered, still uncertain about what I would possibly say.

"Why don't you let me be the judge of that?"

Remaining within the secure confines of the Jeep, I pulled the pink cat-eye glasses out of my purse. I could see recognition across his face.

"Where did you get those?" He asked suspiciously.

"I purchased them yesterday, over at Thrifty Rags on West 21st Street. I'm fairly sure they belonged to Rose O'Brien; the lady killed at the retirement village a few months back."

"She did own a pair of glasses similar to those."

"I'm pretty certain these were hers," I contended with a frown and a nod.

"What makes you think so?"

Drawing in a breath, I held it for a moment before exhaling sharply and spewing forth my explanation.

"This is going to sound crazy because I'm living it and I'm finding it crazy. But I'm not crazy. When I put these glasses on, I experience Rose's death. Not that I actually die, like she did obviously, but I see and feel what happened to her on the day right before she was murdered," the words spilled out in a rambling rush before I could stop myself.

I breathed out a heavy sigh of relief. *There, that wasn't so hard, was it?*

He didn't burst out laughing, which I took as an encouraging sign, at least for the time being. However, I could see the hint of a smirk turning up at the corners of his mouth.

The door to my vehicle opened and the detective leaned in, offering me a hand. I leaned further into my Jeep, away from him.

"Let's discuss this inside," he urged with a nod towards the building.

I sighed and unbuckled my seatbelt. Gathering up my purse and keys, I was escorted into the brick structure by Det. Kendall. Obnoxious florescent lights illuminated the interior, causing a severe strain upon my eyes. My footsteps echoed through the halls as I followed the detective, practically running to keep up with his tall frame. He offered me a seat in his office and then sat down behind his large oak desk, pulling out a yellow legal pad.

My eyes wandered around the stark room. Apart from one commendation for Distinguished Service hanging on the wall, there was nothing else which screamed out this office belonged to the youthful looking detective. There were no personal pictures or mementos anywhere to be found.

"How long have you been a detective?" I asked, trying to assess his age.

"About a year and a half."

"Hmm."

"So, Mrs....?" he paused, waiting for me to fill in the blank. Condescension seeped from his phony smile.

"Ms., Windsor. Marlie Windsor. I'm divorced," I replied, holding up my left hand, minus a wedding ring. Why I'd felt the need to add that, was beyond me and inwardly I cringed.

I jerked my hand down into my lap, embarrassed by my idiocy. I could feel my cheeks begin to tingle with warmth.

His shoulders moved up and down in controlled amusement.

"Ms. Windsor, why don't you tell me about these glasses. You say you see Mrs. O'Brien's death, when you put them on?"

Again, with the slight smirk, along with some degree of raised eyebrows. I very much wanted to smack it right off his face. I, however, abstained. Assaulting a police officer was not on the agenda for the morning. However, at this point, I was considering penciling it in for later in the week. Condescending, little shit.

"Listen, I am not crazy. I am not drunk. And I don't do drugs. I want to establish that right now," I barked, shaking my finger at him.

"So, you're a psychic then?"

"Ah, no," I shook my head and gave him a look of disgust. "Don't be absurd!"

"You don't believe in psychics?"

I threw my hands up.

"I don't believe in any of this shhhhtuff, which is why I told you, 'this was probably not a good idea'."

"If you don't believe in any of this, then why are you here?"

I let out an exasperated sigh.

"Ever since I found these glasses and put them glasses on, I've been experiencing Rose's death. The only thing I can attribute this 'awaking' to," I made air quotes with my fingers, "is a bump to the head I took yesterday morning when I slipped on a patch of black ice."

"Have you been checked for a concussion since you've started having these hallucinations?"

"They are NOT hallucinations," I growled, "I only have these weird images when I put on Rose's glasses."

Interlacing his fingers, he set them on the desk and leaned forward. "Fine, tell me what you see when you're wearing the glasses."

I could tell he was just humoring me, but I was here, so figured I might as well give him my story, unbelievable as it may be.

"When I put them on, I, or rather Rose is sitting in a rocking chair, knitting. She has a ton of cats around her. She gets up to make tea for her friend, Ethel and while she's in the kitchen, she gets stabbed in the back."

"We are already aware of all of this," he acknowledged, rapidly tapping his index finger on his desk, apparently irritated.

"Did you know it was a woman in red high heels who killed her?" I asked smugly.

Det. Kendall sat back in his chair and gave me a slight side eye.

"What makes you think a woman in high heels killed her?"

"Because as Rose was dying, she saw a woman in high heels standing next to her. Then the woman told her, 'rest in peace, Rose', before Rose died."

This time the detective leaned all the way back in his chair, his arms across his chest. "And what did this woman look like?"

"I have no idea," I answered with a slight shrug and shake to my head.

"What do you mean, you have no idea? You just said that Rose saw a woman standing next to her after she was stabbed," he asked indignantly.

"Yes, but she was on the floor, dying. She only saw the woman's shoes. Red high heels with a pointy toe."

The smirk.

He nodded his head. "Ok, well, if you have another vision or if Rose shares any further bits of information with you from beyond the grave, please feel free to call me."

He reached across the desk and handed me his business card.

Glaring at him, I snatched the card from his hand, dearly hoping I'd given him a paper cut with the thick cardstock.

"I told you this wasn't a good idea," I threw over my shoulder as I departed, grumbling all the way to my car.

It was highly probable before I had even gotten to my vehicle, Det. Jace Kendall had been on the phone, telling the officer at the front desk to call the guys with the straight jackets. Either that, or he and his cronies were peeking through the blinds, laughing at my back as I sulked to my vehicle.

I slammed the door shut and put the glasses on. Cute ol' Rose was staring back at me again in the rearview mirror. The scowl on her face matched my own, as if to tell me I hadn't tried hard enough.

"Oh, don't look at me like that," I moaned, ripping the glasses off my face, and tossing them to the passenger seat in a huff.

Needless to say, I was not in an entirely pleasant mood when I arrived at The Back Porch. On top of my encounter with the irritating detective, traffic was backed up for several exits on the highway and I only needed to make it to the next one. I hate traffic, especially stop and go traffic. I will go twenty miles out of my way, just to keep moving.

Helen must have been waiting impatiently for me to arrive. She was nearly jumping out of her skin when I finally walked through the door.

"So, what did they say? Was the detective single and good looking?"

I scowled at her.

"Uh oh," she whispered aloud.

"Det. Kendall… told me to call him if Rose decides to share any further tidbits from beyond the grave," I answered, slumping into my chair. "And I have no idea if the little shit is single."

"Is he short?"

"No, quite the opposite. Except I think he's only about twelve years old." I rested my head in my hand and let out a sigh of exasperation. "I guess I can't blame him. The whole thing is kind of ridiculous when you look at it from a sane person's point of view."

"So, you're just going to let it go unsolved?" Helen admonished.

"What else can I do? That boy child detective didn't believe a word I said."

"We'll just have to think of something else then," Helen promised.

The bell on the front door tinkled softly, indicating we had a customer and put a halt to our discussion of Rose O'Brien, Det. Kendall and what to do about her death, at least for the time being.

3

Surviving all the other perils set before me on my quest, I was ready to claim my hard-fought after reward. I was on the verge of recovering the cache of hidden gems, from within the secret compartment of the old, weathered desk. Slowly opening the drawer, golden light ebbed forward, I squinted through the brightness. No, it wasn't golden light. A swarm of brilliant, jeweled bees erupted from within, flying wildly around my head. The infernal, metallic buzzing was making my head ache, with a dull thud. I waved my hands frantically, trying to shoo the irritating insects away from my face. The intense humming would *not* go away.

Through one eye, I again peeked at the cell phone lit up on my nightstand. Minute rays of sunlight were peeking in through the slit in my bedroom curtains, bathing the room in a faint yellow glow. I groped for the annoying piece of electronics, knocking something from the nightstand to the floor. I'd worry about it later, when I got up.

"This had better be good," I protested, hoarsely though sleep infused eyes.

"I figured out what you can do," Helen chattered. Her voice was way too perky for this early, sun devoid hour.

"And what is that pray tell?"

"You still have your CNA license, right?"

"Yes, I just renewed it in January," I confirmed, with no remote clue as to what she was getting at.

"You should go down and volunteer at Willow Glenn. You can snoop around some, basically with permission, and see if you can gather any pertinent information. I mean I guess you don't need your CNA license, but it can't hurt."

Even at this early, o-dark thirty hour, my brain registered this as downright brilliant.

"Not a half bad idea," I conceded.

"I figured you'd appreciate it," Helen replied smartly.

In my mind, I could see her triumphant smile on the other end of the conversation. I envisioned her sipping her early morning coffee out on the front porch, watching the sun rise in the east.

"I do. Could this *not* have waited until I got to the shop though?" I sniveled. "I think that you come up with these ideas late at night just so you can call and wake me up."

"Wah, wah, wah. In the immortal words of John Wayne, 'we're burning daylight'."

Leave it to Helen to quote The Duke, even at this gawd-awful hour of the morning.

"Helen?"

"What?"

"Tomorrow is Saturday, if you call me before 9:00 a.m., I'm going to drive over to your house and set it on fire."

"I'll just have Trevor eat you. Bye, Grumpette."

"Trevor loves me," I responded quickly, before she could hang up on me.

Trevor is her enormous and very hairy Malamute. He is also a bazillion years old and couldn't eat anyone if he wanted to, since he no longer has any teeth.

I clicked the red button at the bottom of the screen to end the call. What did she expect? I am not an early riser, not that I'm much of a night owl either, but two days in a row before 6:00 a.m. Sheesh.

Peyton, once again, sat in the doorway; his head cocked to the side. I glared down at my adorable fur ball from bed and pleaded, "Can't this wait another hour?"

I patted the mattress and he jumped up, snuggling next to me. "Good, boy."

I made a mental note to give him something special when we got out of bed. I snuggled back down beneath the warmth of the blankets and closed my eyes.

After my divorce, my younger sister, Darla, had shown up with a tiny bundle of cuddly, black and white joy. She'd even named him; Peyton, she declared, after the greatest quarterback to set foot at Mile High Stadium, although *I* would debate this point.

And before you go telling me it's blah, blah, blah stadium this week, any true Bronco fan will tell you, it will *always* be Mile High. End of discussion!

Anyway, Peyton is all bark and no bite. He'd definitely alert you if someone was breaking into the house with his incessant barking. However, if the thief offered him a treat, he'd help them pack your stuff up and carry it to the getaway car. Fickle little bastard. Don't get me wrong, I love that adorable, little mutt, but he's a two-faced, little shit sometimes.

An hour or so later, I leisurely rolled out of bed finally ready to greet the morning, only to holler out in pain. Beneath my now aching foot, was a crushed pair of cheap reading glasses. I was beginning to think glasses were becoming the bane of my existence and I cursed every pair as I limped off to the bathroom, a variety of profanities flowing from my lips like an open spigot.

Thirty minutes later, with hair and makeup done, I headed to the kitchen to grab a quick bite. Scrambling a couple of eggs for myself, I threw an extra one in for Peyton, his reward for letting me sleep in an extra hour.

Tossing my dishes into the dishwasher, I grabbed my shoes and headed out the door.

On my way down to The Back Porch, I did as Helen suggested and drove up to Willow Glenn Senior Living, on the far north side of the Springs. The grounds for the institution were mammoth and stretched over several acres. A black rod iron fence enclosed the meticulously kept complex.

The facility consisted of three separate areas. There was an Independent Living area, where patients lived on their own with minimal assistance in separate cottages, along the south side of the property. At the center, was the Assisted Living portion, a six-story condominium looking building, for those needing slightly more care. The Skilled Nursing portion, for residents requiring managed care, stood alone on the north edge of the property.

I rang the buzzer at the security gate and inquired about volunteering. Moments later I was allowed through and proceeded up the long driveway. The administration offices were on the first floor of the Assisted Living complex.

They were extremely grateful for the much-needed help. I was introduced to the woman in charge of volunteers, who led me to her tiny but immaculate cubicle. Personal pictures decorated the panels of her small space, along with an assortment of pictures colored by a child. It was a far contrast to the detective's barren office.

The familiar nursing home odor settled into my nostrils, reminding me of why I had stopped working as a CNA. I chose to keep my license updated as something to always be able to fall back on if times necessitated it.

"We are always happy to have volunteers, especially one with a CNA license," the woman beamed, an excited quiver in her voice.

She continued in a more subtle tone.

"We've had a problem getting staff and volunteers since one of our residents was murdered last October. I have to disclose that," the woman named Lucy divulged, offering me a chair. "One new staff member wanted to sue us after they were told there was possibly a murderer wandering about."

She eyed me closely, seeing if I was going to renege on my offer to volunteer. Not today, Lucy, not today. I have a murder to solve.

"A murder?" I asked, feigning any previous knowledge of the incident, flattening my hand against my sternum.

Leaning forward, she continued in a softer hushed voice, "Sweet older lady, Rose O'Brien. She was such a dear. She'd always go up to the Sniff, when one of her friends was moved up there, to read to them or visit with them fairly often."

"Sniff?" I asked, completely confused.

"Oh, I'm sorry, Skilled Nursing Facility (SNF), we call it Sniff for short. And that Rose, she could knit up a storm. She'd won our annual knitting contest for the last four years straight," she told me, pointing to a flyer on her cubicle wall, for this year's competition. "I do miss her so. She was just the sweetest thing."

"And you say she was murdered? Who would murder a sweet old lady?"

Lucy glanced around cautiously, to see if anyone was listening to our conversation, "Just between you and me, I think it was Bernice Wallace and her husband, Ernie, who did her in. They'd been eyeing Rose's apartment for years. I don't think her body was even cold, when they stormed in here requesting her unit, as soon as it was made available. Reminded me of a pair of vultures circling a rotting carcass in the desert. It was downright unnerving."

Inwardly I recoiled, *who would want to live some place where someone was murdered?* My disgust must have been apparent on my face as Lucy remarked, "I know, right?"

Lucy pulled several different forms from a small tan filing cabinet behind her desk and handed them to me. I filled out all the necessary paperwork and gave her a copy of my CNA license. She then gave me instructions that I could attend some training the following Monday morning and from there I'd be assigned some simple tasks to start. I would be volunteering two days a week (I still had a business to run after all).

Thanking her, I made my way to my Jeep and drove through the complex, acquainting myself with the layout of the property while searching for Rose's unit. The facility was enormous. Making my way back to Voyager Parkway, I headed towards downtown. Weaving my way through side streets and avoiding the highway at all costs.

My mood today was much better than it had been yesterday when I'd met with Det. Kendall. So splendid in fact, I stopped off at the bakery on Fillmore and picked up a box of heavenly pastries, for a work filled day at the shop.

The smell of fresh baked goods permeated the car: gooey bear claws with their hint of almond, plus several chocolaty decadent morsels. I figured I owed Helen since I'd threatened her this morning, after waking me at such detestable hour.

"I brought fat pills," I called out, the bell on the door tinkling, announcing my arrival. I wandered back into the break area, the box of decadence in hand.

"How did it go up at Willow Glenn?" Helen asked, washing her hands, and gazing lovingly upon the box I held in my grasp.

"Great. I start with some training on Monday morning and by the afternoon, I'll be given a few tasks to help out. The woman I spoke with, told me they haven't had any luck getting staff or volunteers since Rose's murder."

I set the lavender gluttonous box down on the counter. Once opened, the smell of sugar and deep-fried dough tantalized our senses. We each took a pastry and continued with our conversation, talking between sweet mouthfuls of baked goodness.

"I guess until they figure out who killed her, people don't want to chance coming across the perpetrator," Helen reasoned. "I wouldn't want to work there with a killer lurking about."

"Lucy, the volunteer coordinator, also told me about this couple who had been wanting Rose's unit. She compared them to vultures vying for the spoils," I informed my business partner.

"Ewwww, who would want to live in a house where someone was murdered. Talk about bad mojo."

"That's what I thought, too. I wonder how many times people have bought a house where a murder was committed and didn't even know it?"

Helen started typing on her keyboard, "I wonder how many states require that disclosure when selling a property?"

I could see her eyes scanning the screen. "Hmmm, this article says most states require any violent death be disclosed."

"Humpf, nothing had to be disclosed to the Wallace's," I added. "They knew Rose was murdered in her apartment. And Lucy told me her body wasn't even cold before they were knocking on the housing administrator's door, requesting her unit as soon as it was cleaned up and available. I can't even imagine."

Helen shivered. "They sound like a creepy old couple. I wonder if they decorate like the Munsters or the Adams."

I pictured the inside of Rose's cute, comfortable apartment, now looking like a mausoleum, drenched in dark black draperies and various sinister creatures lurking in the shadows, cobwebs hanging in the corners, the smell of death and decay suspended in the air.

"I have them on my list to check out while I'm volunteering down there."

"Try and sneak of picture of them to show me what they look like," Helen begged.

Her demeanor turned serious.

"You need to be very careful while you're down there," Helen warned, "don't be too conspicuous. We don't need you alerting the killer you're looking for them. Don't ask too many questions, either. Try to keep a low profile."

My mind tried to keep up with all the random advice my business partner was directing my way.

"Are we really having this discussion?" I asked, somewhat in a daze.

While we talked about it, the whole thing seemed so surreal and fantastical. "I feel as if I'm having an out of body experience."

"You *are* having an out of body experience of sorts, I would say," Helen offered.

She had a point; it just didn't happen to be *my* body or *my* spirit which was floating around.

At this point, I was wishing I could go back in time and make the decision just to go straight to the shop, the morning I found Rose's glasses, instead of Thrifty Rags, and not immerse myself in this unfortunate mess. Then again, if I hadn't, the police would still believe it was a robbery gone wrong and not be aware of the unknown female assailant responsible for Rose's death. I felt as if Rose had picked me to help bring her killer to justice. Somehow, I couldn't let her down.

4

I spent the weekend trying to determine the best course of action to take once I started volunteering down at Willow Glenn. Since I really had no idea what I was looking for, the best I could come up with was to just wing it. Keep my mouth shut and my eyes and ears open.

Still having a closet full of scrub tops, I picked out a black one with pink piping, threw it on with a pair of black slacks and headed out, on Monday morning.

There were only two other people in the room when I arrived for my orientation, both were young women who looked to be in their teens. We were given magnetic name tags and were instructed to wear them whenever in the facility, to identify us as volunteers.

Sitting through the morning training session, I struggled to keep my eyes open and stay focused. The heat within the room was stifling and I used one of the provided manilla folders to fan myself. I hate the cold, but the heat in the place was too much, even for me.

It was the standard stuff you get at any new hire orientation. This, however, was for volunteers, the basic do's, and don'ts, what is and isn't allowed. After a while, the woman up front began to sound remarkably similar to Charlie Brown's teacher in all those old cartoons, 'wah wah woh wah wah'. She was not an inspiring instructor and droned on for half the morning, adding to my sleepy state.

When the session was over, as my first duty for the day, I was given the assignment of filling water pitchers. Images of my first CNA job crept into my mind. The antiseptic smell of Anne Arundel General Hospital permeated my memory. I had wanted, so badly, to be a registered nurse back then. My how times have changed.

I had just stepped into the corridor with a wobbly, metal cart when I glanced up to see Jace Kendall at the end of the hall. I could tell he was just as surprised to see me, as I was him. He moved towards me in an expedited manner, his jaw clenched tightly.

"Det. Kendall, what are you doing here?"

Taking me by the arm and ushering me away from everyone, "I was just going to ask you the same thing?"

"Well, you didn't believe me, so I came to see if I could find further evidence to give to you," I answered through gritted teeth, shrugging out of his grip and glaring at him.

"How did you even get in here? This is a closed retirement facility. Only staff and visitors are allowed on the premises."

"Staff, visitors and *volunteers*," I answered smartly, pointing to my name tag and sounding more chipper than I had intended. "I am a volunteer."

"Since when?"

"Since Friday."

Raised eyebrows.

"I will have you know; I am a licensed CNA," I boasted proudly. "I am completely qualified to volunteer here."

He crossed his arms over his chest, "And just what do you hope to discover while volunteering here?"

"My passion for working with the elderly again," I sighed, placing my hand over my heart.

His narrowed eyes told me that Det. Kendall wasn't amused with my smartass answer. "If there is a killer wandering around this facility, they aren't going to appreciate you snooping about and asking questions."

"I'm just here looking for red pumps. I have no intention of interrogating anyone," I told him. "And I thought the maintenance guy was your chief suspect."

"Don't believe everything you read," he replied. "Now, you seem like a nice enough lady, but you need to go back to whatever it was you were doing, before you got this wild notion."

"I was running a highly successful vintage boutique, until I bought those 'charming' glasses which belonged to Rose O'Brien."

"Then go back to running your business and let the professionals handle this," he directed sternly.

"How can I let the professionals handle it when you're not even looking for the right suspect?"

"Maybe, I'm here looking for a woman in red heels."

"So, you believe me?"

"I didn't say that. However, you did give me something else to think about," he answered, tapping the side of his head. "I need to consider every possible angle."

I exhaled sharply.

"If you'll excuse me, I have water pitchers to fill. It was nice talking to you, detective," a sardonic tone punctuated my statement.

I left him standing in the corridor, as I attended to my duties.   Just because I had ulterior motives, didn't mean I wasn't going to fulfill my obligations as a volunteer. I have an impeccable work ethic.

Pushing my cart around the hallways, I collected and filled water pitchers, exchanging light chitchat with the residents. Subtly, I tried to check out the residential units through the windows in patients' rooms. Unfortunately, the independent living cottages were too far off in the distance and were surrounded on the back side by a six-foot wooden fence, allowing me no view to the nearby dwellings.

During lunch I planned on strolling through the area, trying to see if I could locate Rose's old unit and maybe get a peek inside. Thankfully with our average three-hundred days of Colorado sunshine, the walkways were clear of any remaining snow or ice. There would be no Flying Wallendas today.

I casually walked down the sidewalk, taking in the charm of the cottages within the retirement village. Many of the residents were snuggled inside their warm homes with this recent bout of cold weather we were experiencing. Smoke billowed softly skyward, here and there, from an occasional fireplace; no doubt, keeping the inhabitants cozy. There was no one in sight, walking the streets of the complex, except for myself. From my experience, most elderly people didn't like the cold any better than I did.

I found the address for Rose's unit and did a quick survey of the street, to make sure no one was watching me. Tiptoeing up the soggy lawn, I peeked in through the front window, hoping the Wallace's weren't at home.

Uh oh… I suddenly found myself face to face with the new occupant; a rather burly looking gentleman in a white, stained wife-beater, who I assumed was Ernie Wallace. The disarrayed mass of gray thinning hair on his head, poked out in several different directions. His chin was covered in a layer of bristly, gray stubble. Narrowed eyes bore down on me.

"What are you doing peeping into my house?" The older man yelled at me through the paned glass, while knocking frantically on the window.

"I'm so sorry," I apologized, loud enough for him to hear me as I took a step backwards, "I assumed this unit was empty."

"Well, as you can see, it isn't. So, move along, Missy. And, get the hell out of my flower beds, you're stepping on my damn crocuses and tulips."

I was indeed NOT stepping on his damn crocuses and tulips. However, retreating gingerly from the flower bed, to avoid his precious spring blooms, I turned around to find Det. Kendall sitting in a blue unmarked sedan on the street out front, laughing and pounding energetically on his steering wheel.

As I am want, and habitually inclined to do, I presented him my middle finger and an accompanying dirty look, before trudging back to the nursing facility, to finish up my volunteer hours and head for the shop.

"How was your first day of volunteering?" Helen asked. "Did you discover anything new?"

I gave her my 'I don't want to talk about it' look. Shedding my winter coat and gloves, I plopped into my chair, letting out a deep sigh of exasperation.

"That bad?"

"I ran into Det. Kendall, who told me to let the professionals handle it. I was also yelled at by Ernie Wallace when he caught me peeping through his front window. Which, in turn, was witnessed by the detective, who proceeded to laugh at me from his car."

Helen couldn't hide her amusement behind her grin, "I supposed you flipped him off?"

"Of course, I did," I admitted.

As I said, it *is* a habit I have. My middle finger seems to have a will and a mind of its own, presenting itself at random and not so random moments.

The door chimed and as Helen would say, Mr. tall, dark, and handsome walked in, except for the tall part. He wasn't short by most people's account, but tall to me is over 6'2" and this guy was pushing 5'10", max. His medium brown hair and blue eyes would make most women swoon. I, however, am not most women.

"May I help you?" I asked, rising to greet our new customer.

"I'm seeking an appropriate gift for my aunt's birthday. She adores antiques and anything aged." He pronounced it 'awnt' instead of 'ant' as most of the people I associate with do.

I considered throwing a jab Helen's way and offering *her* up for sale, but I held my tongue. This guy didn't appear as if he would have much of a sense of humor, so I slipped into my professional persona.

"I'm Marlie," I offered, as I extended my hand.

"Artie Watters," he replied, returning my hand-shake.

I escorted him around the shop, pointing out various unique and interesting items, offering background information on them. He admitted he didn't know much about antiques or vintage pieces and deferred to my expertise. Eventually, he settled on a 7-piece decanter set in a stunning green by Murano. I offered to giftwrap it and have it ready for him in about twenty minutes.

Directing him to the coffee shop across the street, I told him I would bring it over, if he wanted to enjoy a cup of black gold while he waited. He agreed to wait for me at Rosco's.

Wrapping each piece of the set carefully and boxing it, I chose an elegant paper with small pink flowers and tied it all up with a lovely bow and sprigs of baby's breath.

Carrying the tastefully wrapped package (if I do say so myself) across the street, I placed it on the table where Mr. Watters sat straight backed, one leg crossed over the other, and reading the local paper. All he needed was a British accent and lit pipe to achieve a Sherlock Holmes vibe.

Ruffling the newspaper and then folding it back neatly, he stood and pulled out a chair for me.

"I took the liberty of ordering an almond mocha for you, upon the advice of the barista, of course," he stated, pointing at a second cup with my name on it.

Olivia, the barista, smiled from behind the counter and waved. She knew my favorite was her special almond mocha with extra whipped cream.

"Thank you," I replied, taking the chair he offered.

"Thank you, for all of your assistance with my aunt's gift. I think she will find it delightful. And this presentation is remarkable, truly a work of art," he remarked, delicately fingering the bow atop the package.

My heart swooned slightly at the compliment. Okay, so maybe I wasn't completely immune to his charm.

We chatted over coffee with him doing most of the talking. He had recently arrived from Connecticut (I kinda figured him for the east coast sort) and he had been out house hunting when he'd stumbled across our 'lovely' boutique. He'd decided to drop in and see what we had to offer since he was in dire need of acquiring a gift for his aunt.

"I am certainly happy I did so," he professed smoothly, taking my hand, and kissing the back of it. "You have been of the utmost help. I look forward to visiting your establishment again. Enjoy the coffee. However, I do have a pressing engagement with my realtor, which I cannot be tardy for."

Taking the package and tucking it beneath his arm, he left Rosco's, walked back across the street and out of sight.

"He's a cutie patootie," Olivia commented from behind the counter and then added, "for an older guy, I mean."

He was cute, I had to give him that, but his manner of speech seemed contrived and superfluous. Something about him just didn't set right with me.

I ordered a coffee for Helen, picked out a couple of scrumptious looking croissants and walked back across the street.

"You were gone a long time," Helen remarked with a sly grin, when I returned. "What have *you* been up to?"

The dubious tone of her question was priceless. She was always trying to make more of my encounters with the opposite sex, than what they were.

"Mr. Watters bought me a coffee, as a thank you. So, I sat and talked with him for a while before he left to 'an engagement with his realtor'," I mocked, adding a hoity toity accent to the last part and holding up my hand, pinkie extended.

"He's…"

"Yes, I know," I interrupted, "tall, dark and handsome. He's as phony as a three-dollar bill."

"Really? Why do you say that?"

I told her about my skepticism and the general vibe he gave off, of putting on airs.

"I'd be surprised if he ever came back to our 'quaint and charming boutique', I think was how he put it."

We both giggled, though I did appreciate the description he'd provided for our shop. Maybe I could bribe one of our clients into adding the description to a review on our website and social media page.

"Wait," Helen waved her arms excitedly, "what did it look like inside?"

"Inside what?" I asked, confused. "Rosco's?"

"No, Rose's apartment. Was it as creepy as we had talked about?"

I snorted.

"No, for the brief glimpse I got of the inside, it was nothing out of a horror flick. And Ernie Wallace was definitely not cutting the heads off his tulips and crocuses and placing the stems in a crystal 'vaze'," I laughed continuing with my hoity toity accent.

"Too bad, it would have been cool, in a creepy sort of way. Don't you think?"

"It would definitely add a whole new dimension to this weird drama, that's for sure," I concluded.

I drove home in the darkness, since we hadn't done the leap forward time shift thing yet, to Daylight Savings. Peyton greeted me with his wagging tail when I opened the door. There is nothing quite comparable to the love of a crazy mutt to make your day better.

Pulling a frozen dinner from the freezer, I popped it into the microwave. I hadn't done much cooking since my son, Hub, had left for college up in Boulder, over a year ago. Maybe I should consider taking a cooking class for one. Yeah, right, like I had time for that.

After choking down something resembling mac and cheese yet tasting as if it were made of cardboard and glue, I pulled the glasses out of my purse.

For obvious reasons, I'd been avoiding Rose's spectacles since the day I'd encountered Jace Kendall at the police station. I wasn't extremely keen on reliving her death yet again.

Tonight, I grabbed a piece of paper and moved to the living room with a glass of wine. Sitting on the couch, I placed the pink frames over my eyes once more. I was going to pay better attention this time and see if there had been any details I'd missed in my previous encounter and write down everything I observed.

The scene began with me in the rocking chair. I counted the cats again. Yup, seven.

"Achoo." I sneezed. Apparently, my allergy to cats was even active in a vision. *Strange*, I thought as my nose twitched, feeling another sneeze coming on. I rubbed the tip of my nose trying to prevent it from coming and then sniffled sharply.

The knitting in my lap was done in a fuzzy variegated blue yarn and appeared to be the makings of a cardigan. The tick-tock of the cuckoo clock provided its metronome pulse in the background. I glanced around the room, to see if the woman in the heels was visible, no such luck.

Cuckoo, cuckoo.

Walking into the kitchen, I looked from side to side and down the darkened hallway, to ensure no one was lurking about. As I began filling the tea kettle, I felt the sensation of the knitting needles in my back.

This time, while lying there, I realized the killer had pulled one of the needles from out of Rose's back and it clattered to the floor, with a hollow aluminum twang. When it bounced up, it had scraped the side of one of the red shoes, leaving a small streak of blood. I concentrated on the spot, it appeared to resemble a tiny hummingbird. And then everything went dark with the voice telling Rose to rest in peace.

I pulled the glasses off. Aha, I had new information for the boy child detective. This had to be something he was not aware of. It was quite possible even the assassin was not aware of the small drop of blood which could link her to the crime.

To celebrate my discovery, I poured another glass of Moscato and gave Peyton a bowl of milk. We sat there enjoying our reward, for a job well done. I would call on the detective first thing in the morning, to report my recent findings. I doubted, however, he would appreciate this newfound knowledge, considering the source.

5

Letting Helen know what I had observed last night, and that I was going to be a bit late coming in; I drove down to the police department on my way into work. This was always a test of my patience, as I hate maneuvering through downtown. There is ultimately some sort of road closure somewhere down there creating a cacophony of chaos.

True to form, I had to work my way through the maze of closed off streets to get to CSPD. Today they were working on a broken water pipe at the corner of Costilla and Nevada, the recent cold weather wreaking havoc on the Colorado Springs water supply.

After explaining I had information regarding a case, a polite, uniformed officer led me to Det. Kendall's office, deep within the bowels of the Colorado Springs Police Department. When we arrived, Jace Kendall was on the phone and twirling a pen between his fingers. The officer knocked on the window to get his attention.

When the boy detective peered up, he couldn't hide his disdain; that exaggerated eye roll… yeah, it gave him away. He held up a finger instructing us to wait a moment. After several minutes he hung up the phone and motioned us in.

"Detective Kendall, Ms. Windsor here, says she has information on the Rose O'Brien case."

"Thanks, Jenkins."

Det. Kendall motioned towards a chair inviting me to take a seat, "Ms. Windsor."

"I can tell you are so pleased to see me, Detective," I needled, flashing him my most disingenuous smile.

He gave me an aggravated sigh. "What can I do for you?"

"I have some new information for you about Rose O'Brien's murder, Det. Kendall," I announced, then sat and hugged my purse to my stomach.

He stared at me, unconvinced.

"Another visit from beyond the grave?" He taunted, his irritating smirk plaster across his face.

That assaulting a police officer thing was moving up on my list of things to do for the day.

"Nope, same one. I just paid closer attention this time looking for details to the crime," I replied, dismissing his taunt.

"I see. (Insert sarcasm here) And what details can you share with me today?"

Ignoring his sarcasm, I pushed on, "The woman in the red shoes dropped one of the knitting needles after she stabbed Rose. When it fell, the needle grazed her shoe, leaving a small trace of blood that resembled a tiny, little hummingbird."

"A hummingbird?" His jaw jutted slightly forward. Annoyed stare.

"Yes, a hummingbird," I replied with my own look of annoyance. "I'm not a blood splatter expert. The smudge the knitting needle left on her shoe, looked like a teeny, little hummingbird," I answered, holding my fingers up about a quarter of an inch apart.

He pinched the bridge of his nose and closed his eyes. He drew in a breath.

"Which shoe; right or left?" He asked, releasing his fingers in an agitated huff.

I ran through the scene again in my mind. "Left, near the back seam, on the outside of the heel. She's probably not even aware the spot is there."

I pointed to the area on my own shoe where the spot would be.

Det. Kendall jotted something down on his notepad. *Probably a doodle*, I thought. Despite that, I actually did have pertinent information for this case, whether he wanted to believe it or not.

"Look, I understand you don't believe me...and trust me, I don't want to be experiencing this stuff either. It's creepy as fffu... hell."

My save on dropping an F bomb brought out a smile and genuine lighthearted expression from the detective.

Composing himself, he asked, "So, in your vision of Mrs. O'Brien's death, the perpetrator pulled the knitting needles out of her back and dropped them?"

"I only saw one of them dropped," I responded, with a shake of my head. "I don't know what she did with the other one."

He grabbed his chin and appeared to be contemplating something.

"Do you have the glasses with you?"

Nodding, I pulled them from my purse and unwrapped them from their tissue paper.

"May I?" Det. Kendall asked, turning his hand over in request.

Reaching across the desk, I handed him the pink frames. Unfolding the temple pieces, he held the glasses out in front of his eyes, peering through them at a distance several inches from his face.

"So, tell me again what happens when you put these on."

I repeated what I'd told him the first time I'd ventured into his office a few days ago. Only this time, including the new information I had learned about the blood stain on the perpetrator's shoe.

"And you'd never met Rose O'Brien before or been inside her unit over at Willow Glenn?"

"I'd never even heard of Rose O'Brien until the day I bought those glasses. Apparently, I was in Nashville visiting my sister when she was murdered."

Again, he jotted something down.

"You seem to possess a lot of details only the killer would be privy to, Ms. Windsor."

"Or the victim," I offered in biting retort.

"And if I checked in your closet, would I find a pair of red high heels?"

"Yes, you would, except mine don't have a minute blood stain on them," I admitted.

It dawned on me then, he might consider me a suspect. However, I had an iron clad alibi. I had plenty of witnesses to corroborate the fact that I was in Nashville during the commission of the crime.

Det. Kendall handed the glasses back to me and shook his head. "I'm just not a believer in paranormal phenomenon. You have to admit, all of this seems just a bit... far-fetched."

"Yeah? I wasn't a believer either, until a few days ago. If I were sitting on your side of the desk, I'd probably tell me to take a hike. But I know what I'm seeing, and I know it was a woman in red shoes who killed Rose. I can't even begin to explain or understand, how or why I'm seeing what I'm seeing, but I am."

He stared at me for a moment before responding, his demeanor less critical.

"I'll review my notes again and I'll keep all of this in mind," he offered, writing a few things down. "Without something more substantial, it's not much to go on."

"Thank you," I expressed with genuine gratitude, pleased he was taking me somewhat serious now.

An awkward pause filled several moments before he spoke again.

"Are you still going to volunteer down at Willow Glenn?"

"Yes, I am," I acknowledged. "They desperately need the help and as you said, you need something more concrete and substantial."

"You do realize, I could arrest you for interfering with an investigation," he threatened.

"Ha, good luck with that. My lawyer would have a field day with it."

I tried to sound unphased by his intimidation tactic, not sure I had succeeded.

Narrowing his eyes, he asked suspiciously. "Why would you already have an attorney?"

"I own a small business," I answered indignantly, "of course I have an attorney."

Teresa Owen was just a simple, but brilliant, tax attorney; however, the boy child detective didn't need to know this.

"Did you consult him or her before coming down here?"

"No, why would I? I've got nothing to hide," I offered.

He rolled his eyes and shook his head.

There was an awkward pause again.

"Detective, can I ask you something about the case?"

"Sure. I can't say I'll be able to answer it, since it's an ongoing investigation."

"Fair enough," I acquiesced. "I'm confused as to how Rose died. Wouldn't a knitting needle have just caused a puncture wound? How could that have killed her?"

He looked pensive, as if he were deciding how much information he was willing to give me. "Per the autopsy report, one of the needles penetrated her heart. The needle which was pulled from her body, as a matter of fact. She bled out internally, in a matter of minutes."

My stomach turned and I almost threw up all over his desk. Seeing my paled condition, Kendall asked if I wanted some water.

"No, I just need to get some air," I confessed, drawing in deep breaths through my nose and blowing out slowly through my mouth.

Thanking him again, for taking me somewhat seriously AND not calling the state hospital, to come and cart me away, I made my way, unsteadily, to my car.

Putting the glasses on, I pleaded. "Come on, Rose, give me something else. I need your help."

Her sweet face simply stared back at me from within the rearview mirror, gently rocking to and fro, humming her sweet tune.

Removing the glasses, I smacked myself in the head, not believing I just asked a dead woman to talk to me. Banging my head on the steering wheel several times, I wondered, *what was my life becoming?*

I knew from the frown on her face, that I needed to solve this, if for nothing else but my own peace of mind. I knew I couldn't drop the idea without reaching a conclusion. I needed to see this through to the end.

It took me a decent amount of time to deal with how Rose had died, wondering if she'd suffered. I sat in the parking lot, still and quiet. I was more determined than ever, now to solve this.

Righteous indignation or not, I did still have a business to run and I needed the peace only a secondhand shop could provide.

Today I chose to avoid Thrifty Rags (for obvious reasons) and set my sights on Grandma's Closet, for any new and interesting pieces for the shop. Picking up a beautiful specimen of green depression glass, I held it in my hands to see if it would give off any weird vibes or to see if some previous owner would pop into my field of vision, expecting me to solve their murder also.

When nothing happened, I began examining the piece for any chips or cracks. Finding none, I carefully placed it into the cart and began searching the shelves once again for more vintage bounty.

There was something comforting being among all these old and discarded items. It gave me a sense of peace and calm. Darla had never been fond of any of it, claiming antiques and old stuff gave her the 'willies'.

My weakness for depression glass, came from my mother, Linette. Growing up, she had collected any bits of cobalt blue glass which she could lay her hands on. To this day, she had a display cabinet full of her favorite pieces.

She had also adapted garage saleing into an art form. During the summer months, she'd circle all the locations she wanted to hit in the want ads of the local paper. Then she'd get out her map of the city and plot a course, rivaling any Naval navigator on the high seas.

Each week she'd use a different colored pencil to distinguish this week from the last. Every house was given a number, then we would follow the dot to dot on the map, with a final destination being the ice cream shop on Union, *if* Darla and I had behaved ourselves.

With our strict upbringing, it was few and far between, that Darla and I weren't rewarded with the cool, creamy soft serve, at the end of garage sale outings. Our mother just needed to give us the 'look', to get us back in tow, if we ever dared step out of line.

So, over the years, I had honed my skills, expanding my searches from simple garage sales to junk shops, estate sales and with technology, eBay and Etsy, among others. I'd learned how to research pieces on the internet with even the slightest sliver of information to start. And now, I owned a thriving business based on all of it, which had made my mother extremely happy and proud. A point I brought up often to Darla, securing my position as 'mom's favorite'.

6

It was on my second day of volunteering that I had the pleasure of meeting Ethel McDonald, Rose's dearest friend. Compared to Rose's plump cheeks, Ethel was slighter in build with a slim face and significantly more wrinkles than her departed friend.

Evidently, after Rose's death, she'd suffered from severe depression and they'd moved her from the Independent Living section to the Skilled Nursing Facility, when her health began failing. She was sitting quietly in a wheelchair, staring out the window, when I came in to change the water in her room.

"Good morning, Mrs. McDonald," I offered in greeting, hoping to engage her in conversation.

She didn't respond, which left me a little disheartened.

I was putting her water pitcher back on her bed table, when one of the nurses came in, blocking my exit. I waited patiently for her to move.

"Ethel, are we going to have a better day today?" The nurse asked, her hands on her hips.

Ethel didn't respond to her either. The nurse handed her a small paper cup with her medication, along with a small cup of water. Ethel took the tablets, swallowed them, and knocked the cup of water to the floor from the nurse's hand.

"I guess we're not," the nurse grumbled. Turning, she addressed me, "can you clean that up?"

Without waiting for a response, the nurse turned on her heel and left me standing there with an angry Ethel and a puddle of water at my feet.

"Sure," I answered to no one in particular, followed with "and a 'please' would have been nice."

"I can't stand that miserable old witch," Ethel snapped. "If I knew she was going to have you clean it up, I wouldn't have done it. I apologize for my behavior."

"Don't worry about it," I told her, bending down, and wiping the water up with a tissue.

"Are you new?" She asked.

"Yes, this is my second day of volunteering," I explained. "I'm Marlie."

"Mmm, it's a shame Rose wasn't able to get her fired before she died," Ethel continued, going back to our previous discussion.

"Excuse me?"

"My friend, Rose, she was murdered a while back. She and old nurse Cratchit there had some issues. Rose had reported her for elderly abuse on one of the other patients. She was killed before anything ever came of it," Ethel sighed, and her shoulders slumped forward.

"I see," I noted, waiting patiently for her to continue and provide more insight. This was the kind of information I was seeking.

"Now, Grandma, you can't go spreading rumors about people. It's not nice."

A blonde woman, who appeared to be in her early-thirties, had entered the room. She walked over and kissed Ethel on the cheek. Ethel returned the affection, with a soft hug from where she sat.

"It's no rumor," Ethel stated adamantly. "She and Rose were arguing one day, and that witch slapped her."

"Nurse Cratchit?" I asked.

"Her real name is Betty Stallworth," Ethel's granddaughter informed me, then in a whispered tone, "Grandma is referring to the nurse from 'One Flew Over the Coocoo's Nest'".

Ah, Nurse Ratched, usually I'm quicker on the uptake for movie references like that, (humph) missed that one.

"I think she was in cahoots with Rose's daughter, Amelia. Amelia kept trying to get them to diagnose Rose with Alzheimer's, but she was onto them," Ethel declared, shaking a finger in my direction. "It's why she left most of her money to the Willow Glenn Foundation, instead of that horrible, greedy daughter of hers."

The granddaughter, Sarah McDonald, gave an exaggerated eye role. "Grandma, I came to have lunch with you. I didn't come to discuss your suspicions. We've been over this a million times. Rose was killed in a botched robbery. You have to stop accusing Betty and

Amelia of her murder. Now, shall we go down to the dining room?"

Still waving a finger at me, as her granddaughter wheeled her out of the room, Ethel shouted, "Rose didn't have anything worth stealing in her house. You mark my words, one of those two is who killed her. I'd put money on it."

Janine, one of the CNA's on the floor, stopped me in the hallway and nodded towards Ethel and her granddaughter, her blonde ponytail bouncing at the back of her head. "If you get her talking about Rose, she doesn't stop. She has a conspiracy about everything. She refuses to believe it was a robbery gone bad when Rose was killed."

I gave Janine a thumbs up, "Gotcha."

I wanted to tell her that Ethel was right about it not being a robbery gone wrong, except I knew I couldn't. That would generate a whole bunch of questions that I didn't have answers for.

I felt guilty that I was spending so much time away from The Back Porch. A detour through Old Colorado City was exactly what I needed to assuage my conscious. At least I'd feel as if I were a contributing member of the team if I stopped off at Thrifty Rags, to see if they had any new items.

When I stepped through the door, I was greeted by the stale smell of aging relics. I breathed it in, filling my senses with nostalgia. Gretchen's brassy auburn head peeked out from behind a rack of clothing and shouted a friendly hello, her wire framed glasses setting at the tip of her nose.

"Hey Gretch, any new Depression glass come in lately?"

"We have a few pieces, they're chipped pretty badly, though. I kept them to the side for you just in case you wanted to do something else with them. They're on the table in back. If you don't take them, I'll have to throw them out."

She loved to save things off to the side, she thought I might be interested in.

Not only did Helen and I deal in rare artifacts... okay, mostly vintage, and classic pieces, we also did plenty of repurposing and upcycling too. Helen was pretty handy when it came to creating unique pieces from broken bottles, glass and dinner ware.

I eyeballed the selection and picked out three pieces I was sure my business partner and I could find a use for: a pink creamer by Federal Glass in a Sharon Pink pattern and two amber salad plates in what I was sure was a Fenton pattern. The others were too severely damaged or stained to be able to do much with, but I took them, not wanting to see them end up in the trash.

Wandering through the remaining aisles, I found a few more pieces I just couldn't pass up. I set my items down on the counter, waiting for Gretchen to finish in the clothing section.

"I have another pair of those cat-eye glasses that someone dropped off," Gretchen beamed, producing a pair of lenses in a lovely turquoise hue from under the counter, much to my chagrin and horror.

She had no idea, of course, how cringy this was for me. The notion of picking them up, gave me an extreme case of the heebie jeebies. Swallowing my fear, I picked them up and turned them over in my hands.

"Let's see how they look on you," Gretchen prompted.

Of course, she would suggest this.

I slowly raised them up before me and then shoved them onto my face, squeezing my eyes closed as hard as I could.

"Did you poke yourself in the eye or something?" The shop owner inquired.

"Dust," I croaked, was the excuse I gave her for my odd behavior.

I opened one eye and peeked out. Just Gretchen. My eye scanned the room for any spirits who might be clinging to the spectacles. I giggled inwardly, spectral spectacles. Okay so, it wasn't that funny.

Reasoning I couldn't sell the pink pair until I'd solved Rose's murder, I told Gretchen to wrap them up with the rest of my booty. What else could I do? The little boy detective didn't seem to want to look for a woman in red shoes. I felt obligated to figure this thing out for Rose's sake and now for Ethel's.

As I drove down Bijou to The Back Porch, I contemplated how I could investigate Rose's daughter, Amelia, and nurse 'Cratchit'. I needed to find a way to get into their closets to check out their shoes.

Breaking and entering was definitely out of the question. Number one, I'm allergic to prison, plus I didn't think I'd look attractive in an orange jumpsuit. The color wouldn't be so awful. That being said, I am way too short, to pull off a jumpsuit. The arms and legs are always much too long for me. I pictured myself as one of those billowing air people they put in front of car dealerships; it wasn't a pleasant image.

My biggest problem was, I had no idea where Amelia lived. I wasn't even sure if she lived in the state, let alone our city. I could always follow Cratchit after work sometime to ascertain where she lived, I reasoned thoughtfully.

So, the first thing I did when I got to the shop, was pull up Rose's obituary on my computer. Rose was survived by her daughter Amelia Boyd, Amelia's husband, Max, and daughter Chelsea of dat dah dah dah... Colorado Springs.

It was a start. Now, how to find her address? A quick internet search yielded nothing. I decided on my next day down at Willow Glenn, I'd see if I could get some more information from Ethel. As far as I could tell, she was my best lead in garnering any useful information to pass on to Det. Kendall.

"Good gawd," Helen bellowed from the back, sorting through what I'd brought in today, "another pair of those hideous glasses? Have you been checked for a concussion yet?"

"Do you even appreciate what I had to go through to get those? Gretchen must have thought I was nuts," I chided, peeking into the storeroom, and relaying my peculiar behavior down at Thrifty Rags. "It was awful."

Helen snickered and shook her head.

"You *are* nuts, for buying a second pair of these ugly things."

"Are we or are we *not,* a vintage shop?" I asked sarcastically. "Those were high fashion in the 50's, the blingier, the better. I bet if we searched, we could find a picture of someone in your family wearing something very similar to these."

"Yeah, yeah, yeah," Helen rolled her eyes so far back into her head, I thought I may never see them again.

"I wasn't really into the Beatles, but then again, you are *much* older than me."

Much older, being about eight years.

"What?"

"You know...'she loves me, yeah, yeah, yeah'," I sang, belting out the Fab Four song.

Helen rolled her eyes again. "Do you know *why* the Beatles sing that song?"

"No," I answered, shaking my head perplexed.

"So, that *you* won't," she teased.

I gave her the evil eye and slunk back to my desk to sulk. Mental note: I'd have to remember that insult, so I could use on my son or Darla, sometime in the future.

Several minutes later, Helen came in and waved the turquoise glasses at me, "So, are there any spirits attached to this set?"

"Not that I noticed. I asked myself the same question. Yeah, no, no spectacle specters attached to those."

"Excellent! And no more of these bling encrusted things until we sell both pair."

"I can't sell the pink ones until I solve Rose's murder. They might show me something else when I least expect it," I argued.

"Great point. At any rate, as soon as we figure out who the killer is, those pink ones go on the shelf and are up for grabs. Though I can't imagine who would want to buy them."

"I'm sure there are plenty of people out there looking for a pair of those, purely for nostalgic reasons. I will bet you dinner and a gallon of margaritas, we sell *both* pair," I challenged, extending my hand.

"You are on," she accepted, shaking my hand to secure the bet. "How long should we give it?"

I tapped my finger to my lip. "How about nine months?"

"Agreed."

Realistically, it didn't matter if they sold or not. Helen and I could always find an excuse for chips, salsa, enchiladas, margaritas and sopapillas. And not necessarily in that order.

7

It had been an uneventful day at Willow Glenn Senior Living. I did my rounds, hoping to catch some more gossip from Ethel. However, her family was here today, and they had spent my entire shift with her, leaving me no opportunity to speak with her.

As many relatives do, Ethel's daughter-in-law, Rita McDonald, gave me a haughty glare, when I had entered the room. I'd seen this look so many times, from the so-called 'caring' family members. You know, the ones who show up once a month and then treat you as though you were vermin because you hadn't aspired to something greater in life. In their opinion, making you a glorified butt wiper, so to speak.

I ignored her quiet disdain and continued on about my duties. I was not about to let a woman of her ill disposition get to me.

There were several other patients whom I was beginning to grow rather fond of as well. Many of them reminded me of my own grandparents, long since passed. Among them, was a retired Navy captain, who insisted I take him to the top deck to get some sun.

"Thank you, sailor," he told me, when I wheeled him to the window where the sunlight was streaming through.

Giving him a mild salute, "Captain."

He returned my salute with a, "Carry on."

Mary, who was 104, loved to tell anyone who would listen, about her family's life in Kentucky and coming across the plains in a covered wagon, headed to California. Her family had settled in Colorado, when the wagon had broken down, in the small town of Nunn, just north of Greeley. Her stories of growing up on the prairie rivaled any told by Laura Ingalls Wilder. She was just grateful to have someone listen to her, her eyes lighting up as she shared her experiences.

John was a retired WWII fighter pilot, who had flown a P51 Mustang during the war. He would regale me with stories of dogfights and air combat, using his hands as props and sharing his daring maneuvers and aerial prowess. He, too, was grateful just to have someone listen to his tales of glory.

I once read that 'Every time an old person died; it is as if a library burned down'. Never a truer statement was uttered, in my humble opinion.

It was truly an honor and pleasure to provide care for our heroic veterans and pioneers. Working as a CNA could be rewarding and fulfilling at times, although depressing and disheartening at others.

It was difficult watching the elderly and the daily struggles which aging brings on. Be that as it may, it was still wonderful to listen to their stories from the past. The worst was watching Alzheimer's and dementia patients, who no longer recognized their loved ones. The pain the families endured during these times was awful.

After an exceedingly boring morning, I was getting on the elevator, to go down to the cantina and grab an iced tea for the ride to the shop. As the door closed, I was staring down, thinking about all the work I needed to catch up on down at the shop. A woman in a beautiful floral dress and heels walked past… red heels. The doors closed and started down as the image finally registered in my brain.

I began mashing buttons madly, trying to get the elevator to stop and the doors to open. When it finally came to a halt, I tried to pry the doors apart. As soon as I could squeeze myself through the narrow gap, I hit the stairs running.

You would think that living in Colorado most my life, I'd be used to the altitude, but taking the steps two at a time had me sucking wind like nobody's business, a stitch flourishing in my side. I burst through the stairwell door reminiscent of a mad woman, my eyes scanning the horizon for the red heels and the floral dress, which was worn with them. No luck, the woman was nowhere in sight.

My labored breathing began to ease after several minutes as did the pain in my side. Eventually, I straightened and took some deep breaths.

Casually, I started wandering the hallways, seeking the owner of the elusive red shoes. Peeking into many a room I shouldn't and receiving unwanted glares.

I was about to give up when I spotted the woman with the floral dress. Unfortunately for me, she was sitting behind a desk and was on the phone, so I wasn't able to get a decent look at her shoes. I did, however, discover the dress and the shoes belonged to Karen Brighton, the facility administrator, as noted on the nameplate outside her office door.

Remembering what Ethel had shared about Rose leaving a large portion of her estate to the Willow Glenn Foundation, I wondered if maybe Ms. Brighton hadn't sped along Rose's donation, with a fortuitous demise. Could the institution be in financial trouble and needing money?

I called Helen and told her I wasn't sure if I'd make it down to the store, as I had plans to sit in the parking lot and see if I could catch a glimpse of those shoes. She told me not to worry and to find out what I could. I also asked if she could do some digging and see what she could find out about the financial status of Willow Glenn Senior Living.

I sat in my car all afternoon, every now and then blowing into my cupped hands and rubbing them together. March can be a crap shoot in Colorado, one day it might be in the high 50's and the next in the low teens. Today was bitterly cold with a windchill of 10 degrees; it *was* frigid.

Seeing as I'd put off filling my gas tank, because of this cold spell, running the engine for heat was out of the question. Did all sleuths have problems comparable to this? Shivering, I contemplated doing this on a warmer day, although before I could turn the Jeep over, the woman in the floral dress appeared in a heavy winter coat and gloves. Jealousy of her warm attire reared its ugly head and I longed for a warmer coat and gloves of my own.

Following closely behind Karen Brighten was none other than Betty Stallworth, aka nurse Cratchit.

This is where a clone would come in handy. I watched each of them walk to their cars. Which one to follow? I needed to make a decision. Ethel had pretty much accused the nurse of murdering her best friend. However, floral dress lady definitely had a pair of pointy red heels and possibly had a motive.

Decisions, decisions.

It was starting to get dark by the time Karen Brighton and Betty Stallworth had exited the building. Fumbling in my purse, I found a scrap of paper and wrote down the make, model, and color of each vehicle, luckily in this light, both cars were white. From this distance and fading daylight, I wasn't able to make out the license plate numbers of either vehicle, though.

I made the decision to follow whichever of them drove away first, my need for heat being the deciding factor. I was freezing and my body was demanding warmth.

It was at this point, I determined that I didn't make a very competent detective, I needed to up my game. Envisioning myself in a crimson Carmen Sandiego trench coat and hat, I made a mental note to get a small notepad or mini tape recorder to keep inside my purse for any future surveillance.

I considered using the demon inside my phone, but she never returned valuable info. And on the occasion when I had dictated notes, when I went back to read them, I'm pretty sure she only spoke in some old ancient version of English, because none of it made any sense.

Cratchit was the first to back out of her parking space. Another quick mental reminder: if I ever had to address this woman, DO NOT call her nurse Cratchit, it would prove to be most embarrassing.

She turned left onto Voyager Parkway, taking it all the way down to Academy Blvd., other left and down to Union. Following her south on Union Blvd., she pushed through a very orange light at Constitution. Being the law-abiding citizen that I am, I stopped for the glaring red light and watched her taillights proceed on down the road. Keeping an eye on her, I noticed she took a right onto Palmer Park Blvd, the next major intersection. Gunning it when the traffic light turned green, I was stopped again at the next corner. Whoever ran the traffic light system in town needed a swift kick in the as… pants.

While I waited for the oncoming traffic, I glanced across Palmer Park and saw a dinky, little man about eight inches tall, crossing in the crosswalk, in front of me. Doing a double take, I decided I legitimately needed to see a doctor. I squinted; certain I was experiencing a leprechaun sighting. Afterall, I did have this newfound paranormal ability and it was only a few days until St. Patrick's Day. If I were going to be catching leprechauns, I could get used to this paranormal stuff.

As the itty-bitty being hopped up onto the curb and into the light from the streetlamp, I saw it was only a black cat with white socks on his front paws. This was exhilarating and disappointing at the same time. Illusions of pots of gold faded, with the realization that I was experiencing a bout of matrixing and was not crazy. I know, I know, this is probably debatable according to Helen and most assuredly Det. Kendall.

Shaking the image from my head, I turned right to continue my pursuit of the evil nurse.

To my utter disappointment, there were no visible taillights on Palmer Park when I turned the corner. *So much for following nurse Cratchit*, I sighed. I was genuinely proving to be an utter failure at this crime fighting thing. I vowed to rewatch all those outdated reruns of old 70's cop shows, I was certainly no angel of Charlie's.

Pulling under a lamp post on Columbia Street, I did a search on my phone for White Pages; you know that rather antiquated method of finding someone's address or phone number. It gave me options to Find People, Search Address or Reverse Phone Lookup.

When the app opened, I touched 'Find People' on the screen and entered Betty Stallworth's name. Viola, it produced an entry for one Betty Stallworth on N. El Paso Street, only a few blocks away, in the historic Patty Jewett neighborhood. This is an older section of town with charming bungalows built in the mid-20th century and boasts one of the oldest golf clubs in the country, dating back to 1897.

Weaving my way through the back streets of the neighborhood, I found the address on N. El Paso and saw her white Honda parked on the street. I stopped a few houses away and waited.

Okay, now what? I wondered. I did another search for 'Surveillance for Dummies'. All it returned was information on how to easily install security cameras. Apparently, there wasn't a huge market for the book, since I could find no reference to it.

Sitting on the dark street, I surmised that evening, springtime surveillance, for the most part, sucked. It was dark and it was cold. I had to keep wiping away the condensation from my windows to keep eyes on Cratchit's residence. This experience had already taught me a valuable lesson: always keep a full tank of gas.

I was also hungry, and I had Peyton waiting at home. Thankfully, Connie, my neighbor, had agreed to take him for a walk, when I had decided to conduct my clandestine ops.

The only saving grace to this hellish stakeout, was the devilish, handsome stranger who was out walking his massive Rottweiler. He nodded in greeting as he passed the Jeep, his smile was enough to warm every chilled inch of my body. This part of my surveillance, I wasn't going to share with Helen. It would just embolden her more in her pursuit of a boyfriend for me. She'd probably want me to come back and follow him to find an address and access if he were single and within a respectable age bracket.

After another hour of freezing my tushy off, I had had enough and headed towards the hacienda. When I got home, I filled the tub with the hottest water I could stand and submerged myself into the warmth. I smiled as I watched the steam rise, content and sated.

Once I had removed the chill from my flesh, I opened the laptop to see if I could find information on how to conduct surveillance. One article provided some helpful hints, such as: use a vehicle that blends in, limit breaks, avoid distractions.

The vehicle I had covered. Everyone in Colorado owns some sort of SUV, so my Jeep Grand Cherokee wasn't going to stand out. Limit breaks, this one could be a problem with a needy little mongrel waiting at home. Avoid distractions, for example: the urgent need to use the facilities and handsome strangers with killer smiles.

I also found my fingers doing a search for 'breaking and entering' and 'entering through an unlocked door'. Both results ended with jail time if seized, so I quickly decided to choose a different route to investigate Betty Stallworth and Karen Brighton.

Somehow, I needed to get a closer look at Karen's red high heels. I considered tackling her on the lawn of Willow Glenn next time I saw her in those shoes. Envisioning myself knocking the poor woman down, stealing her shoes and sprinting from sight, I quickly banished the idea. I run as slow as molasses flowing uphill, and assault and battery would *also* earn me jail time. Which, as I mentioned before, is not conducive to my health.

I made the decision, since I now knew where nurse Cratchit lived, I would follow Karen Brighton to her residence the next time I left the nursing home.

It hit me that what I needed was a pair of binoculars. I jumped back into the Jeep and popped over to Powers Blvd. I was cruising south when I homed in on Jake's Sporting Goods. Sliding across three lanes of traffic, I headed for my target.

Inside, I made my way to the back where the field glasses were kept inside a tall, glass storage case. There were so many different models and brands to choose from.

I didn't need anything elaborate or expensive, just something to increase my visual distance.

"Can I help you with anything?" A young man, with Nathan on his nametag, asked.

"Nathan, I'm looking for a pair of binoculars."

"I can help you with that. What are you going to use them for? Hunting? Surveillance?..."

"Pft, surveillance, ha… no, bird watching. I've recently taken up bird watching, and I need a pair for that," I lied, stumbling all over my own tongue. I am not a convincing liar.

"I'm a birder myself," Nathan confided, seemingly ignorant of my untruth. "Do you have a reliable reference book? I can recommend a few."

"Yes, I do. I have an excellent one which my friend, Connie, gave me," I continued with my lie. "I don't need anything extravagant, I'm not sure I'll stick with it, you know?"

He seemed disappointed, obviously an avid birder. "Yeah, it's not for everyone. Though, once you get the bug, you'll be searching in every bush and tree to see if you can spot a lifer."

I grinned and nodded, having no idea what the heck 'a lifer' was.

Nathan wrote down several social media pages for me, which involved birding and birding locations within the state. Thanking him, I redirected his attention back to my need for a pair of ocular extenders.

I selected an inexpensive pair of compact lenses, which fit into the palm of my hand, then jumped back into the Jeep. I would check them out when I got home and see what kind of range I had with my new purchase.

Frowning at the glaring gas light which appeared on the dash, I pulled into the nearest gas station and put in just enough gas to tide me over until it was a bit warmer.

Peyton was waiting for me and jumped up on me for his ritualistic petting. I gave him a quick rub to the head and then dumped the bag containing my new binos onto the kitchen counter.

One ripped box and broken Styrofoam packaging later (I'm not known for my patience), I held my new binoculars aloft in triumph.

"These are for catching the bad guys, Peyton," I announced. He glanced at me, from his position on the couch, for about half a second before closing his eyes again, indifferent to my excitement.

I turned off the lights behind me and stepped out onto the balcony. This was going to be a quick test because it was still bitterly cold outside. Choosing an apartment window across the courtyard, I adjusted the wheel on top, bringing the image into a clear and sharp focus. I scanned several of the other windows adjacent to my building. In one of the ground floor apartments, I observed another individual with his own set of spy glasses, peeking at someone in my building. He must have had the feeling you get when you're being watched, because suddenly he turned my direction, and we were staring at one another through our respective pairs of binos.

We stared at one another for several moments before he stepped back into the darkness and closed his blinds. I pulled mine from my face as well and counted over from the left to see which apartment the peeping Tom was in. I'd have to mention it to Connie and have her do some snooping of her own, since it was in the direction of her apartment 'the creeper' was directing his attention.

Happy with my new purchase, I put them on the kitchen counter and headed to bed.

8

Today, instead of filling water pitchers, I was assigned to change out all the linens and make beds; gotta love those hospital corners. I loaded several sets of linens onto my cart and started down the hall, slightly annoyed with the squeaky wheel on the cart I'd chosen. I kept expecting to bump into the detective again, yet so far, I hadn't seen any sign of him since our first run-in over a week ago.

I had fifteen beds to change sheets on, Ethel's room was one of them. While I was in her room, one of the CNA's came in and dropped off some mail for her. Examining a pink envelope, she wrinkled her face and threw the envelope at the trash can. Missing it, the letter fell to the floor.

"Damn it," she whispered gruffly, staring at the discarded letter.

"I'll get it for you," I offered, picking it up and handing it back to her.

She held her hands up as if warding off an evil spirit. "I don't want that thing. I don't want anything from that greedy woman. Please, just take it away and burn it. I don't even want it in my trash can."

Examining the envelope, I noticed it was from Amelia Boyd, Rose's daughter. I casually slipped it into my pocket for inspection at a more convenient time.

"I'll throw it out for you," I promised, crossing my fingers behind my back. I hated lying to her.

"Thank you. She tried several times to get the doctors to diagnose my friend, Rose, with Alzheimer's. Her and crusty old nurse Cratchit."

"I remember you telling me that the other day," I responded.

"I did?" She wrinkled up her face and stared at me, "Are you sure?"

I gave her a nod.

She gave me a slight shrug. "Hmm, I don't remember. It's awful to get old, you can't remember anything. It's going to be a hell of a day when I can't even remember my own name."

Ethel's granddaughter, Sarah, breezed in. She immediately began opening the curtains and letting sunshine flood into the room.

"Good morning, Grandma."

"Good morning, sweetheart. How is your mother today? Are her headaches any better?"

"Not really, they seem to have gotten worse over the last six months."

"I'm sorry to hear that," Ethel told her granddaughter.

"She's doing well today, though. She said she and Mac would be down later. She's having lunch with her friends from the club."

"Which club is that, Sarah?" Ethel asked.

"Those ladies with the red hats and shoes. The one she's been in for years. I think you told her about it, if I remember correctly."

119

"Awww, yes. I remember them. I used to be in the same club, a long time ago," Ethel responded and seemed to be remembering her time in the club, as a smile crossed her wrinkled lips.

I busied myself making the bed, so I could give them some privacy once I was done. The comment about the red shoe club hadn't escaped my notice either. I'd have to do some digging into Rita McDonald now too.

"Grandma, the annual knitting contest is coming up," Sarah commented as she folded an afghan in half and placed it over Ethel's lap.

"I don't want to knit anymore," Ethel told her, crossing her arms over her chest with a huff.

"But you love knitting," her granddaughter reminded her.

"I *used* to love knitting. I loved sitting with Rose over a cup of tea and gossiping about all the old broads who live here and betting on who'd kick the bucket next. I just don't find pleasure in knitting any longer."

"I think Rose would want you to enter the contest," Sarah urged her grandmother.

"I'm NOT entering the damn contest. If you're gonna pester me about this, then you can just leave," Ethel shouted angrily and pointed to the door.

"Alright, alright, I won't mention it again," Sarah ceded, holding up her hands defensively.

I finished making Ethel's bed as quickly as I could and scooted out, not wanting to get in the middle of a family squabble. I had seen the flyers posted around about the knitting contest and hadn't given it a second thought. It made me sad to think that Ethel had lost her passion for knitting upon her friend's demise.

Heading for the ladies' room, I pulled out the envelope and punched Amelia's address, from the return label, into my phone. I was half tempted to open the letter and read it. I started to throw it into the trash but reconsidered, something inside wouldn't let me throw it out, so I tucked it back into my pocket for the time being and returned to making up beds in the remaining patient's rooms.

Amelia Boyd lived on the northwest side, in the Mountain Shadows subdivision, right along the foothills.

Maybe I couldn't get into her closet, however I could stake out her house and see if she ever came out wearing red high heels and then devise a plan to closer examine them.

The next hour dragged, and I watched the minutes on the clock slowly tick by, while waiting for my volunteer hours to end for the day. Not bothering to stop and change clothes at home, I reluctantly hopped on the highway and headed down I-25 taking the Woodmen exit then heading west towards the mountains.

The majestic Rockies loomed before of me. One of the best things about living in Colorado Springs, is the view. From almost anywhere in town, you get stunning views of Pikes Peak and the front range. It was something I never grew tired of and marveled at each morning.

As I entered the Mountain Shadows development, nostalgia jerked at my heart strings. This entire area used to be part of the Flying W Ranch, a working cattle ranch where they served chuckwagon dinners and did a live country music show. Unfortunately, the ranch was destroyed in the Waldo Canyon fire last year in 2012. I remember watching the fire from across town and remarking to my sister that the Flying W was gone, as the fire rolled over the mountainside. It had been heart wrenching, watching a piece of my childhood be destroyed. Thankfully, soon afterwards, plans were made to start to rebuild the ranch. Even now, new vegetation has begun dotting the landscape with random patches of green.

Shaking off the melancholy, I took the next left onto Amelia's street. Luckily, there was a park up the block, so I could sit there in my car without being too conspicuous. Today though, I had plenty of gas in the tank to keep warm. Checkmark in the 'pro' column.

Amelia's was a large, dark blue two-story house with a neatly manicured front lawn and flower beds flowing with springtime blooms. There were no cars in the driveway at Rose's daughter's house. They were either at work or parked in the garage. Only time would tell, so I waited patiently.

I reached for my new binoculars, only to remember, they were still sitting on the kitchen counter. I knew I was forgetting something this morning. I groaned, another black mark on my investigation resume. It was a good thing I wasn't applying for any PI positions; I'd never get hired with my dismal record.

As I waited, it dawned on me I had no clue as to what Amelia looked like. How was I even going to know if it was her when she showed herself? I wracked my brain trying to think of a way around this slight flaw in my plans. This put another tick in the 'con' column of my sleuthing curriculum vitae. It was a given I'd never get hired to work at a PI company with this depressing review.

With Ethel's intense dislike for the woman, I could hardly ask her anything about Amelia. And I didn't want to draw unwanted attention to myself by asking anyone else. I decided to play it by ear and see where this led, fly by the seat of my pants, as it were.

After an hour or so, the sun started its descent behind Pikes Peak, shrouding Colorado Springs in a blanket of darkness and cold evening temperatures.

I was cold, tired and hungry when I started up the Jeep and headed for home, with no sign of Amelia Boyd.

The whole, not bothering to stop and change clothes thing; had cost me. Peyton must have been upset with me for not coming straight home, because he had turned his water dish over in the kitchen. Unbeknownst to me, until I walked across the floor in my socks, soaking up the excess water and giving myself soggy feet.

"You little menace," I snapped, "I hate wet socks!" Peeling them off, I tossed my damp booties into the washing machine, vowing to throw a load in before I headed to bed.

That crazy mutt had no shame. He came over, sniffed my feet and then walked to his overturned bowl, giving me a look indicating he needed some more water.

I narrowed my eyes and glared at him. Putting his paws up on my thighs, he wagged his tail, begging for me to pet him. Bending over, I grasped his head in my hands and leaned in, "You, are a little shit."

His tail flailed back and forth even faster. He knew I couldn't stay mad at him for long. I rubbed his head and filled his water bowl, instructing him *not* to turn it over again or suffer the consequences. Just what those consequences were though, was a mystery to both of us. Each of us acknowledging, I was all talk when it came to disciplining him.

125

Fixing myself some dinner (a glass of milk and six Oreos), I sat down with a notebook. I made a list of people of interest which included: Betty Stallworth, Karen Brighton, Amelia Boyd, Rita McDonald, The Wallaces (Bernice and Ernie), and the maintenance man mentioned in the news article the other morning. I was certain he wasn't the killer, however.

I now knew where Amelia and Betty lived, so I would need to follow Karen Brighton home next and see what I could discover about her and those red high heels of hers.

As with, Betty Stallworth, I used the White Pages to see if I could find any information on where Rita McDonald lived. Unfortunately, there was no listing for her, and I didn't have any idea of her husband's name, leaving me no other name to search for. Maybe I'd get lucky and find an envelope with their address on it in Ethel's room too.

After I had compiled my list, I scooted down to Connie's, so she'd be aware of the peeping Tom, from across the courtyard.

"I saw some guy from one of the ground level apartments peeping through a pair of binoculars in this direction."

"I thought I saw some sort of reflection from that direction the other night," she complained. "I bet it's the creepy old guy in 102 over there. He's always eyeing the girls at the pool in the summer too. He needs to be taught a lesson."

We devised a plan.

Connie slipped across the darkened courtyard and waited beneath the window in which I had seen 'the creeper' in. I went back upstairs and watched in the darkness to see if he'd spy on anyone this evening.

At 9:15, I saw him appear in his window, binoculars in hand. He glanced my direction. This time I was further back tonight and hidden within the shadows of my apartment. He turned his attention towards our building. I dialed Connie's cellphone and then trained my binos on his window again. Watching intently, I saw Connie pop up right in front of him and yell out 'Booga, booga,

booga'. She screamed loud enough that I heard her up in my apartment, even with the balcony door closed.

I slid the door open to hear Connie roaring with glee from down below.

"I scared the crap outta him," she hollered up at me and laughed even harder.

She was still hysterical when she arrived at my door, out of breath from the havoc she had wreaked on 'the creeper' in 102.

"Did you see the look on his face? Old geezer got caught with his pants down, so to speak," she chuckled. "He went flipping backwards over his bed and then crawled out of his room."

She opened the balcony door and yelled, "Serves you right, you creep."

Her laughter was contagious, and we sat on my sofa holding our stomachs and sides. Peyton burrowed under a side table and looked out at us as though we were aliens.

9

I couldn't stake out Betty's, Karen's or Amelia's houses twenty-four hours a day, or every day for that matter. And I still had no clue where Rita McDonald lived or how I was going to investigate her. The only thing I knew was she owned a pair of red high heels, according to what I'd heard Sarah mention.

Between running my business and volunteering, Peyton was beginning to take offense. One afternoon, I was about an hour later than normal. I came home to a box of shredded tissues. Bits and pieces of torn tissues lay strewn across my living room. He sat in the middle of the mess with an expression that warned, 'I shouldn't be left alone too long to my own devices'.

"You little, freakazoid," I scolded.

Pointing to his bed, I sent him off to think about what he had done. He sulked off, his tail between his legs and his head hung low.

Circling twice on top of his bed, he plopped down and stared at me with his big dark eyes. This lasted all of five minutes. Before long he was jumping up on the couch next to me and snuggling in, worming his way back into my good graces; damn, he is a lovable little mongrel.

At the next opportunity, I followed Administrator Brighton down Highway 115, to her house down in Cheyenne Meadows. It was a small ranch style home, with white siding and overgrown junipers covering the yard. A landscaper she was not.

I wasn't sure if she knew I had followed her, because she remained in her car for about ten minutes before getting out. For all I knew, maybe she was waiting for the song on the radio to end. I mean I've done that myself on numerous occasions. You never want to waste an excellent jam.

This was the first chance to use my new binoculars while doing surveillance. I'd finally gotten into the habit of keeping them in my purse, with their compact size. Then, I'd have no excuse for leaving them behind.

When she did finally exit her vehicle, I zoomed in and focused. I couldn't help but notice the size of the woman's feet. Noah could have borrowed one of her shoes instead of building the ark; and as I had mentioned to Helen, the killer had small feet. Sasquatch was, most definitely, not the culprit. Disappointment rose as I realized my search for Rose's killer would have to continue. But at least I'd be able to check one person off my suspect list.

From what Helen had been able to discover so far, the facility was not in any kind of financial trouble. So, I could only assume, Karen Brighton probably had nothing to do with expediting Rose's death for any monetary gain.

After that, I alternated my days between Betty and Amelia's homes, when I wasn't playing catch up at the store. I felt guilty that I had been relying on Helen so much, to run our business, while I tried to solve Rose's murder. She never complained and was extremely supportive of my quest, always encouraging me to keep at it. I didn't ask, but I think she wanted justice for Rose as much as I did.

Fortunately, volunteering had let me figure out Betty's work schedule, so I didn't have to squander time at her residence when she wasn't there. Though, I still hadn't figured out how I was going to uncover if she had a pair of red high heels, with a tiny bloodstain on them, hiding in her closet. It was highly improbable she'd ever wear heels with her white nursing scrubs, so I was in a quandary.

Because Rita's visits to see Ethel were few and far between, and with no particular schedule, I was still unsure of where she lived or how best to investigate her. Most of the time, she visited her mother-in-law on the days I wasn't volunteering.

On my way home from The Back Porch this afternoon, I drove down El Paso Street, hoping to discover something... anything, about Betty Stallworth, which could prove or disprove her involvement with Rose O'Brien's death.

I pulled over when I saw a teenage boy wheeling the trash to the curb in front of her house. Once he had gone back inside, I exited the car and meandered down the sidewalk, casting a sideway glance into the large, black trash can.

On top of all the white garbage bags was a shoe box. I had seen enough cold case shows to know, that once the trash was on the street, the cops could pick it up and sift through it, sans warrant.

Snatching the box from the top of the trash, I hurried back to my car, hoping to discover Betty's shoe size from the side of the box. Realizing it wasn't empty, I opened it. Major blunder!

I choked, coughing violently, on the stench emitted from a pair of smelly, old, gym shoes, which lay inside. Fumbling with the lid, to trap the offensive odor back inside the box, all I managed to do was spill the foul-smelling sneakers out and onto the passenger side floorboard.

Rushing around to the other side of the car, I grabbed the shoes, to return them to the trash receptacle.

At this very moment, Betty Stallworth walked out of her house and got into her car. I jumped behind a bare hedge in an attempt to keep her from seeing me. Watching from my hiding place, I saw as she started up her white Honda and drove away, leaving me hiding in the cold, still clutching the stinky footwear.

Running back down the street, I threw the shoes and the now empty box into the trash and raced back to the Jeep. I grabbed the bottle of hand sanitizer I keep in the console, only to discover it was empty. Gagging, I drove home, all my windows open to air out my vehicle, and was summarily rejected by my small ball of black and white fur. He was having nothing to do with me and the atrocious smell, which clung to my hands and clothes.

I felt as though I had to shower a dozen times to remove the foulness, I had unwittingly subjected myself to. All in a failing effort to find the supporting evidence I needed, to solve the crime I was investigating.

Lesson learned? Pack some latex gloves, trash bags and zip ties into the car. Also, replace the empty bottle of hand sanitizer. Thinking about the list of sundries, I realized this was everything a serial killer might keep in their inventory, along with lye, a bottle of bleach and a hatchet.

I did a mental head-slap and shook my head. *I'm going to bed.* This investigating thing was becoming more trouble than it was worth.

It was on the fourth or fifth day of staking out the Boyd residence, when a blue van pulled into the driveway. A well-dressed man, roughly my age, exited and opened the back hatch. He struggled to remove a collapsible wheelchair. Setting it next to the passenger door, he helped a disabled woman into the seat.

I rolled my window down and listened closely, straining to hear their conversation.

"Well, Amelia, what did the doctor say?"

The woman squiggled her bottom back into the seat with a concerted effort. "She told me the MS is in remission, though it could change and flare back up at any time. But I'm satisfied with the visit today. Today has been a good day."

The gentleman leaned over and kissed her on top of the head. My guess was this was her husband, Max.

Amelia had Multiple Sclerosis. Seeing the effort it had taken for her to reposition herself in the wheelchair, I realized she could not possibly have killed her mother.

Processing the new information, I started the car and pulled away from the curb. A school bus was coming up the street and stopped in front of me. I stopped, waiting for the children to exit and cross the street. I glanced to the seat next to me and saw the letter which Ethel had recently rejected.

A tiny nagging feeling inside, told me to return the letter to Amelia. When the school bus started up again and passed me, I pulled up in front of her house.

I was filled with trepidation as I rang the doorbell and took a step back, my heart thumping loudly in my ears. I could hear movement inside and waited for the door to open. Amelia Boyd answered and stared out at me from her wheelchair.

"Mrs. Boyd, my name is Marlie Windsor, I'm a volunteer down at Willow Glenn."

She appeared puzzled.

"How can I help you?"

"I just wanted to return this to you," I conveyed, offering her the letter I had in my hand. "You sent it to Ethel McDonald, but she asked for it to be thrown away. Something told me I needed to give it back to you."

She pulled back from the door and motioned me in. I opened the door and handed the pink envelope to her.

"Please, come in." Amelia wheeled into a lavishly decorated living room and directed me to the couch.

I felt as though I had stepped into the cover of Better Homes and Gardens magazine. The room was tastefully decorated in light blue, cream, and gold. Expensive furniture filled the spacious living space and a baby grand was tucked into a far corner. For the extravagance that the room exuded, it still maintained a homey and warm sense.

"Thank you," she sniffled, tears began to trickle down her cheeks. "I realize she doesn't care for me; she thinks I was after my mother's money. This is a birthday card that my mother had signed for her. It was among her belongings when they let us in to go through her things. I know my mother would want her to have it."

"Maybe after your mother's murder is solved, she'll be in a better place to receive the card," I suggested.

"I hope so. For some reason she is convinced I wanted an inheritance. The truth be told, I was the one who suggested mom leave an extensive amount of her estate to Willow Glenn, since they had taken such outstanding care of her, up until her death that is."

"Ethel is telling everyone you kept trying to convince the doctors that your mom had Alzheimer's."

Amelia giggled through her tears.

"No, Ethel is the one who is in the beginning stages of Alzheimer's, not my mother. I think she's confusing me with her daughter-in-law, Rita."

"I see," I nodded. "So, then did your mom and nurse Crat... um, nurse Stallworth have issues?"

"Yes, *that* was my mom. She believed Betty was abusing one of the other patients and they got into a shouting match. Betty lost her temper and slapped my mom."

"And Betty still has a job?" I asked, astonished.

"No formal complaint was ever filed by the other resident or by my mother. I'm not sure if she was written up or given a warning of any kind."

I pondered this information for a bit.

"Well, thank you for seeing me and I hope someday Ethel opens her heart before it's too late," I offered, standing to take my leave.

"Thank you for returning the card. I'll see if I can get it to her daughter-in-law or granddaughter maybe, so they can give it to her. Maybe she'll accept it from one of them with an explanation."

Amelia saw me to the door, and I drove home in silence. It was heart breaking to discover Ethel was in the beginning stages of Alzheimer's. As a CNA, I'd seen plenty of patients with that terrible disease. It was awful to see them deteriorate, some of them declined so quickly it was scary. While others languished for years not recognizing their loved ones or knowing who they were.

Once home, I called my mom and dad down in Florida, just to ease my mind. They spent the colder months down in the warmer clime of the Keys; while spending the hot, humid months of the south up here in Colorado. It was hard being so far from them for part of the year, but Darla was in Nashville and would go down to see them every few months. And I made it down that way at least once each winter, if not more.

I crawled into bed that night feeling lonely and completely lost. Peyton must have sensed my sadness and curled up next to me instead of his usual side of the bed. It was quite a while before I drifted off into a restless slumber, thoughts of Alzheimer's and dementia, occupying my thoughts.

10

So far, my endeavor at Willow Glenn had proven mostly unfruitful. Karen Brighton had been eliminated as a suspect. Amelia was also out. Her MS wouldn't have allowed her to walk, let alone walk in heels similar to the those I'd seen repeatedly in the replay of Rose's death. I hadn't been able to eliminate nurse Cratchit, Rita McDonald or the Wallace duo. And no one else jumped out as a suspect, so my options were dwindling.

Curiously, a few days ago, I'd bumped into Ernie Wallace out in the courtyard. This time he wore a wrinkled gray flannel shirt over his stained wife-beater. He obviously remembered me peeking through his window, because he gave me the stink eye for several minutes before going on his way. If looks could kill, he definitely had the look of a killer.

Thus far, I had not had the pleasure of meeting Mrs. Wallace. From the rumors I had overheard though, I probably should avoid crossing paths with old Bernice. She was not popular among the Willow Glenn crowd. Whispers I heard included the words: manipulative, conniving, and witch, except with a capital 'B'. But does any of that make a person a murderer?

Today, I would see if I could coax any information out of Ethel about her daughter-in-law. I already knew Rita felt I was beneath her by the way she'd look at me, when she visited with Ethel. I determined my best approach would be to show interest and concern over Rita's increasing headaches.

"Good morning, Ethel. How are you today?" I asked.

"I'm alright," a soulful sigh escaped her lips.

"Just alright?" I prodded.

"Yes, Rita and Sarah were going to visit today, but Rita is having another migraine and Sarah offered to stay home and take care of her mother."

"I'm sorry to hear that. Would you like for me to check on her on my way home?" I offered.

"Oh, how sweet of you, but they live in a gated community though and they don't let anyone in without prior notice. Very strict security at their place," Ethel assured me.

"Which gated community?"

She looked as if she were in thought but then began banging her palm against the side of her head.

"Oh, what's the name of it? One near Garden of the Gods, up on Mesa Road," she put forth, ceasing hitting herself in the head.

I wasn't sure what to do about her hitting herself. I'd definitely report it to the nursing staff, but should I mention it to Sarah the next time she visited?

"Camel View Condominiums," Ethel shouted out. "I knew I'd remember it."

Swanky neighborhood. I'd never be able to get in there. But at least I had a place to start in my surveillance of Rita McDonald.

"Well, I hope she feels better soon. Is there anything I can do for *you*?"

Glancing around the room, checking to see that no one was listening. "Can you steal me another cup of Jello?"

I smiled and gave her a wink, "I'll see what I can do. Any particular flavor?"

"Anything except lime. I hate lime," she told me, sticking out her tongue.

A quick trip to the nurse's station and I returned with a cup of orange Jello for Ethel.

"Enjoy," I told her, as she ripped the lid off the container and jammed a spoon in.

Stepping out into the corridor, I was confronted by none other than Bernice Wallace. She was an amazon of a woman, built very much like her burly husband, with almost identical gray stubble on her chin.

"I hear you've been peeping in my windows," she grumbled, towering over me, "And stepping on my husband's flowers."

"Um.. I.. I understood your unit was empty and I was interested in what they looked like inside. I'm terribly sorry if I upset your husband or yourself," I apologized.

My neck was starting to ache from straining to look up at her.

"I've got my eye on you," she told me, pointing at her right eye. "You better be minding your p's and q's."

She strutted off down the hallway, her posture erect and her large shoes making a resounding clomp, clomp in her wake.

What the heck were p's and q's?

As I was leaving, Lucy, the volunteer coordinator was waiting to talk to me.

"Marlie, we had a complaint from Bernice Wallace. She claims you were harassing her husband the other morning while she was off at her water aerobics class."

How was I going to explain this without sounding like a fool?

"I'm guessing it was some sort of misunderstanding between you and him?" Lucy suggested. "Bernice loves to make mountains out of mole hills."

"Well, as a matter of fact, it was. I was walking during lunch and was curious as to what the Independent Living quarters looked like inside. I thought the unit I picked was empty and I peeked in the window, only to find myself face to face with Mr. Wallace. I apologized to both himself and his wife. I didn't mean to cause any trouble," I confessed.

Lucy waved her hand, "I figured as much. Those two enjoy creating chaos where there isn't any. Just keep out of their way and I'd avoid the Independent Living area all together just to be on the safe side."

"I understand."

"Have a good evening, Marlie. We'll see you Thursday for the knitting competition."

Hopping into a golf cart, Lucy headed off towards the Assisted Living building.

So, Rita McDonald lived in a gated community. Which meant I'd stand no chance of doing any worthwhile surveillance there, security would be tight. I figured I might have to wait on a side street, near their neighborhood and try to follow Rita once she was out in public. But first things first, I'd need to find out what she drove if I had any chance of following her.

My phone buzzed in my pocket. Pulling it out, I saw it was Helen. I had hardly gotten out a hello when she began chattering away in an excited tone.

"They arrested the maintenance guy, Frank Dennison. It's all over the news. They found him in Florida. Apparently, he was trying to pawn several items belonging to the residents at Willow Glenn. They'd had him under surveillance for several weeks and were waiting for him to try and fence the stolen items. He was wanted on burglary charges and suspicion of murder.

"When the cops were taking him into the station in Boca Raton, a reporter asked him about Rose and her murder. He told her 'I may be a lot of things, but I ain't no killer' and that he'd never harm another soul, especially Rose O'Brien. He swore up and down he wasn't guilty of killing her."

"Because he 'isn't' guilty of her murder. I'd bet money on it. Though it seems as if he has other crimes to answer for," I replied.

This latest development made me even more determined to find the murderess with the red heels. I had so many questions for so many people. It was daunting realizing most of them would undoubtably go unanswered.

I would have dearly loved to have been the proverbial fly on the wall, at the jailhouse down in Florida, to garner any snippets of information from his interrogation. Certain I wouldn't be able to weasel any pertinent information out of the detective, I threw the idea onto the trash heap.

Unfortunately, I would have to wait on news reports coming out of the Sunshine State, to get any information on Mr. Dennison and his arrest. Though I knew in my heart and from looking through Rose's glasses, he wasn't responsible for her death. Or was he? Could he be working with the woman in the red heels?

I'm sure I had some of the same questions for him the police did. My main one was, had he seen anything the day Rose was murdered, which might point to the woman in the red heels? Then again, he may not have even been in the residences the day Rose was killed. Yet, if he wasn't, then why would he be a person of interest? The questions just kept piling up, it was frustrating to say the least.

There had to be something I was missing. I replayed what I'd seen over and over again in my mind, while I filled water pitchers. But to no avail, nothing of any significance jumped out at me.

I spied Betty Stallworth, in the hallway, I took notice of her feet. They were small, small enough to have fit into those red heels, however, it was hard to tell for certain with the bulky nursing shoes she wore on her feet at the moment.

Too bad it hadn't been her shoes in the box from the trash several days ago, it would have answered at least her shoe size. I almost gagged again, thinking about the atrocious smell emitted from those dirty old gym shoes. It reminded me of a day when my son, Hub, was in middle school. Several of his friends had come over to play video games, leaving their shoes at the bottom of the steps. The basement smelled remarkably like a locker room, from the smelly feet and body odor of four to five, 13-year-old boys. Disgusting was putting it mildly.

I foresaw another day of surveillance in my future. I needed to discover if the vile nurse owned any red pumps with a bloodstain on the heal. And I needed to devise a plan to investigate Rita McDonald somehow.

I stopped outside of the gates to Camel View Condominiums and peered inside. There was a small building just inside the fence with a security guard keeping watch over who came and went from the complex. He eyed at me suspiciously.

Holding my phone to my ear, I pretended to be pulled over and on the phone. It's against the law to drive and talk on your phone in Colorado (as I'm sure it is in several states), so I would use that as an excuse if he came over to question me.

I wasn't sure what I was hoping for, maybe Rita would pull through the gate in front of me, either coming or going and I'd discover what she drove. But then I recalled what Ethel had said about her not feeling well today and Sarah staying home with her mother.

The homes inside the complex were more of patio homes then condominiums. I found the name for the housing project didn't reflect the development accurately. I would have chosen a better name. The Patios at the

Mesa sounded better in my opinion. I mean the homes did have a fantastic view of the Kissing Camels in the Garden of the Gods, but Camel View made me think that I'd was looking at the rear end of the humped animal.

An olive-green Range Rover exited the gated community. Too my astonishment, it was driven by Sarah McDonald. But she was alone in the vehicle, so any chance of catching a glimpse of Rita in red high heels was nil.

At least I knew I had the right gated community and made plans to return the following evening.

At home, I turned on the 5:00 news, dearly hoping that Heather Skaggs at Fox21, would provide further information regarding Frank Dennison's arrest. Unfortunately, the news cast seemed to be just a repeat of what Helen had relayed to me earlier. All the channels had the same information, which was basically nothing that would help me with my undertaking in solving Rose's murder.

Later in the evening, I put the glasses on again. I had to be missing something. I would have to relive her death over and over, until I figured out what it was.

Check out everything, I reminded myself as I started down the macabre path of death again. Rocking, knitting, cats… same as before. When I stood to go into the kitchen, I looked out the front window to see what the weather was like. Sunny and from the looks of it, not a cloud in the sky – good ol' Colorado.

On the street, with just a hint of it showing, I noticed a gray car. I was unable to determine the make or model from this angle. *Could this be the killer's car?* I hadn't considered before that maybe the killer *was* there to rob her. Maybe she was seeking something specific Rose owned. The house had, after all, been ransacked. Or was it just a car on the street and it had nothing to do with Rose's death?

Pain in the back, dropped tea kettle, falling to the floor, woman in red shoes… same ol', same ol'. The voice, 'Rest in peace, Rose.' Darkness.

I took the glasses off, disheartened. I had more questions tonight, than I had when I woke up this morning.

How did those police officers do this, day in and day out? It was exhausting and frustrating trying to resolve this riddle.

Something sparked in my head, I was missing something, and I was getting frustrated. I put the glasses on again, watching it unfold for the dozenth time. 'Rest in peace, Rose'. I took a breath and then I understood. Perfume, I smelled perfume. Before everything went dark, I breathed in deeper, drawing the scent into my nostrils to remember for later. There was a fruitiness to the scent. I knew that smell, but I could not place it at the moment.

Where had I smelled the perfume before? I started ticking off places in my mind: the shop, the bank, the grocery store, Willow Glenn, the police station. I couldn't recall, but I knew I had encountered the scent recently. I decided it must have been at Willow Glenn, I *was* dealing with Rose's murder after all. For smell being your most nostalgic sense, it was gravely failing me when I needed it the most.

I ambled off to bed still trying to recall when and where I had come across the scent. It was hours before I finally drifted off to sleep, none the wiser.

11

Upon waking, I still could not remember anything else about the perfume I had come across, during my most recent visitation to Rose's death. Rushing through my morning, I prepared for another day of volunteering down at Willow Glenn.

I guess I'd gotten used to Helen's early morning wake up calls, because I forgot to set my alarm. If this wasn't solved soon, I was fearful that Helen might find a new business partner. Though, I must say, she seemed as interested in solving this crime as I was.

Pulling through the drive-thru at a local coffee hut on Voyager, I ordered an almond mocha (not remotely as good as Olivia's) and a chocolate croissant. I gobbled the croissant and washed it down with the sweet rich coffee.

Of course, being in a rush, I hit every light red on my journey north to Willow Glenn.

When I arrived, the dining room had been cleared of tables and set up for the knitting competition, with chairs in rows facing a portable stage. Many of the residents sat in the rows up front, with others sitting in their wheelchairs at the ends of the rows. Tables had been set up to display all the entries, from the gaggle of contestants. There were brightly colored afghans with varying patterns, as well as baby layettes, sweaters, and scarves. All were beautiful and showed the care and love put into each piece.

Three judges, selected from different art supply businesses around town, were carefully examining and critiquing each piece and writing notes on index cards. Once complete, they handed all the cards to Karen Brighton, who would tabulate the votes. Once all the votes were counted, winners would be announced, and prizes awarded.

A conglomeration of guests and staff began filing into the dining room. To my amazement and confusion, many of the staff and guests were dressed in red, in honor of Rose. Red had been her favorite color. The vast majority of them were wearing… red heels.

I breathed out heavily, a sigh of frustration.

People moved around the room, engaging in conversation, commenting on the weather and the friendly rivalry taking place with the current competition, filling the room with a noisy din.

My eyes darted around the room, examining every pair of red shoes, searching for the telltale bloodstain on the left heal. Dozens of feet moved within my field of vision. There were so many red shoes, it was making my head spin. I had about given up…

And then, there they were, the red heels with the minute hummingbird blood stain, along with the scent of the perfume I'd been trying to recall. I reached for my phone; it wasn't in my pocket. Ugh, of all days to leave my cellphone in the car. I had left it in the console on the charger, not thinking I'd need it during the competition.

Quietly and discreetly, I exited the dining room and headed off in search of a landline to call the boy child detective. I hurried through the corridors to the administrative offices, knowing for sure I'd find a phone there.

I slipped into one of the rooms down the hall and picked up the receiver. Punching in the number for CSPD, I waited for it to start ringing.

"Det. Jace Kendall, please," I whispered quietly when the police department answered.

It rang again. Once. Twice.

"Pick up," I implored into the receiver.

"Kendall."

"Detective, this is Marlie Windsor," I uttered softly into the mouthpiece, "you need to get down here to Willow Glenn."

"And why's that?"

"I found Rose O'Brien's killer and she's here at Willow Glenn right now. We're at the knitting comp…"

I saw her in the mirror behind the desk, but before I could relay anything further to the detective or duck, she hit me with a folding chair across the back of my head. Everything started spinning as I fell forward across the desk.

I came to on the ugly brown and orange carpeting, prevalent in retirement homes and hotels, my arms bound at my sides and a gag in my mouth, dearly hoping it wasn't a dirty sock from one of the residents.

Sarah McDonald was sitting in the chair she'd hit me with. From where I was on the floor, the evidential blood stain taunted me.

"You're pretty nosy for a volunteer. When the old bat of Ethel told me that you were the only one who listened to her about Rose, I started keeping my eye on you. Problem is I don't know who you called, so I'll have to wait and see who comes looking for you and dispose of them as well."

The idea of her going from a single murder to a serial killer in the blink of an eye, threw me for a slight loop. In for a penny, in for a pound, I guess.

She stood and began pacing back and forth, the tiny hummingbird flying by at my eye level.

"How'd you figure it out? I was *so* careful. I really hadn't intended on killing Rose, I liked her," Sarah rambled.

"She was just so unreasonable when I asked her to drop out of the competition. 'Ethel wouldn't want me to drop out of the competition just so she could win,'" she mocked Rose's voice.

"And damn Ethel, with Rose out of the way, she would have won the damn knitting contest too, but she refused to compete. That old bitch has come in second place my entire life, not a winning bone in her frail, old body," Sarah blathered on.

"I gave her a chance to be a winner and she threw it back in my face by not competing. I should have killed *her* instead of Rose. Rose was a competitor. Rose was a winner. Why couldn't she be my grandmother?"

Had I not been bound and gagged on the floor, I would have pummeled the woman standing over me and given her a piece of my mind.

"Sarah, *you* killed Rose?" I heard Ethel ask. I moved enough to see her in her wheelchair in the doorway.

"No, no, no," I screamed in my head, wishing Ethel away. Struggling furtively, I rolled onto my side.

Sarah approached Ethel and put her hands on the arms of the chair, then leaned down face to face with her elderly grandmother. "Yes, I killed your precious Rose. I'd gone to her house to convince her to let you win the miserable knitting contest for once. Of course, she wouldn't do it. I went into the bathroom to try and calm down after she'd told me no. When I came out, she was starting the water for your afternoon tea. While I was in the living room, I grabbed her knitting and began pulling it off the needles and unraveling it. She couldn't win if she didn't have anything to enter. I was furious, I had one of the needles in my hand and her back was to me. I snapped. I grabbed the other one and plunged them into her back. I was soooo angry, I tried to stab her again, but I dropped one of the needles. When I realized what I had done, I knew I had to make it appear as if a burglary had taken place. So, I wiped my fingerprints away and then ransacked her cottage just before you showed up and discovered her body."

I was waiting for her to add that she'd have gotten away with it too, if it hadn't been for those meddling kids and their dog, when Jace Kendal appeared behind Ethel, gun drawn.

"Step away from your grandmother and put your hands in the air," the detective ordered.

Sarah backed away slowly and raised her hands above her head. With all my might, I spun on my hip and knocked her feet out from beneath her. The dainty hummingbird took flight and Sarah landed in a heap on the floor next to me, with a loud grunt.

A mad scramble ensued as she tried to right herself. Tackled by the detective, she let out a slew of profanities when he rolled her onto her stomach and slapped those shiny silver bracelets around her wrists. Another officer was seeing to Ethel, making sure she was alright. Her pale face suggested she was in shock to discover her granddaughter capable of what she'd done.

Once Det. Kendall had cuffed Sarah McDonald, he knelt down next to me, removing my gag by peeling the tape away from my mouth.

I spit out the tissues that Sarah had stuffed into my mouth before placing the tape over it. Bits of tissue stuck to my tongue. I kept flicking my tongue inside my mouth trying to remove the remaining pieces of fluff.

"That take down was completely uncalled for," he reprimanded me.

"Maybe… but it sure felt great," I declared with a grin, still bound in tape. That bitch must have used every roll of packing tape in the nursing home because I resembled a transparent mummy. Thank goodness, she hadn't wrapped my head, I wouldn't have a single strand of hair left if she had.

He smiled, a genuine smile from the boy child detective. Reaching to one of the desks, he grabbed a pair of scissors and released me from my sticky transparent cocoon.

Helping me remove the miles of tape Sarah had wrapped me in, he asked, "How did you figure out it was her?"

"I didn't until I saw the blood stain on her shoe. I was watching every pair of red shoes walk by, I felt as though I was watching a race at Talladega or a ping pong match.

"When I spotted them, I was going to use my cellphone, but I'd left it in the car. So, I began searching for a regular phone."

"You scared the hell out of me when the line went dead. I grabbed a couple of guys and rushed up here as quickly as I could," he confessed.

"I didn't realize she was on to me, so I wasn't prepared when she whacked me from behind with the chair," I stretched my neck and rubbed in between my shoulders.

"She could have killed you. I told you to let the professionals handle it."

"Pft, you'd still have an unsolved murder on your plate, if I'd have let you handle it. You didn't have any reason to suspect Sarah McDonald was the killer. Nobody did."

"Well, you're not wrong there," Det. Kendall admitted.

It was at about that moment when Karen Brighton muscled her way into the room, demanding answers. Jace Kendall turned me over to a couple of paramedics and then took her to the side. Her arms flapped about akin to a wild turkey trying to take flight, as she badgered him for an explanation.

Det. Kendall insisted I go to the hospital in the ambulance, telling me he would be down there later to take my statement. I kept trying to assure him I was fine, but he wouldn't hear of it.

A team of paramedics hauled me onto a stretcher and loaded me into the back of an ambulance, I was poked and prodded all the way to the hospital. I was adamant about not letting them start an IV, getting slightly indignant that they wanted to charge me for something I absolutely did not need.

"I was hit with a chair for crying out loud," I argued. "Why in the hell would I need an IV? Unless you're going to start pumping me with pain killers, then you can forget it."

The paramedic rolled his eyes at me. "Fine, suit yourself." He sat back, crossing his hands over his chest, for the remainder of the trip to the hospital.

I was kind of miffed, that my injuries hadn't warranted a speedier ride, with lights flashing and sirens blaring. What's the point of being taken to the hospital in an ambulance, without all the pomp and circumstance?

12

After a slew of tests, x-rays, and an MRI, it was determined I had sustained a grade 2 concussion from my run in with Sarah McDonald. The ER doctor was a pleasant, older gentleman, by the name of Dr. Wood, who voiced the same objections I had, to the paramedics starting an IV. After treating me and prescribing some pain killers and muscle relaxants, for my raging headache and neck pain, he patted the stretcher and wished me a blessed afternoon.

Sitting on a gurney in the ER, I waited impatiently for the doctor to release me. However, I was informed I was to stay put until the boy detective arrived. It seemed as though several hours had passed, before Jace Kendall peeked his head in through the curtains surrounding my bed.

"How are you feeling?" He inquired.

The chair which Sarah McDonald had hit me with, had my head pounding like a freight train and my neck stiff and aching.

"As well as can be expected after being hit with a chair, I suppose," I groaned.

He stood there awkwardly. Silence teetered back and forth between us like a child's seesaw.

"Is this where I get to say, 'I told you so'?" I asked, shattering the quiet.

"I guess it is."

I, however, refrained. I didn't want to alienate the detective, just in case I might need a friend on the force in the future. Wow, try saying that three times fast.

Kendall continued, "Sarah's version is spot on with what you relayed to me a few weeks ago, right down to the hummingbird blood stain on her left shoe."

I puffed up my chest triumphantly and smiled. "Case solved."

I brushed my hands together, indicating a doneness with the whole affair.

"Now it will go to trial. It wouldn't surprise me if her lawyer tries to plead insanity."

"I'd say he or she would have a strong case, I mean who kills someone because their grandmother doesn't win a knitting contest for Pete's sake?"

He shrugged, "It wouldn't be the strangest case I've ever worked, but it's damn close. Between the victim and the crime, and you and those damn glasses, this has been a true oddity.

"I figured I should be the one to take your statement. It might be awkward trying to explain how you knew so many of the details of the crime."

He had a point. I tried to envision sitting on the witness stand answering questions to the effect. I almost snickered out loud imagining *the* scene unfold.

Once the detective finished with my statement, I was free to leave.

At Dr. Wood's suggestion, I called Helen to pick me up. He didn't feel I should be driving after the blow to the head and sporting a moderate concussion. I had been transported by ambulance and my car was still at Willow Glenn, so it was a moot point anyhow.

"What the heck happened?" She asked once I had gingerly pulled myself into the passenger seat.

"I found the murderess and then she found me," I moaned, struggling with my seatbelt.

Helen gave me an appraising glance and helped me buckle myself in.

"You don't look so hot. I'd say you could use a margarita or two."

"Sounds amazing to me. I'd say more like three or four margaritas are in order. Concussion be damned. I think I need to get drunk."

"Where do you want to go?

"Anywhere with tequila and amaretto," I told her, closing my eyes, and leaning back into the seat. My entire body ached from my waist up.

A silence filled the inside of the car as she waited for me to explain what happened. I remained mum.

"So, are you going to tell me who killed Rose or not?"

Turning my head to the left, I peeked at her through one eye, silent and then grinned.

"Damn you," she protested loudly, pulling away from the curb with a huff.

On our drive to procure and consume vast quantities of alcohol, I relayed my version of discovering that it was Sarah McDonald, Ethel's granddaughter, who had killed Rose after Rose had refused to drop out of the competition and let Ethel win.

"All because of a knitting contest?" Helen asked.

"She appears to be a highly competitive young woman," I replied, sipping on my Italian margarita, and munching on chips and salsa.

"Well, now she'll be competing on the prison soccer team. She won't be needing high heels in the slammer."

I gazed at Helen through blurry vision, wondering if there truly was a prison soccer team. Those medications the doctor gave me for pain, were starting to kick in. Hallelujah!

**

171

The next day, I was asked to come down and speak with D.A. Victoria McAdams. Jace Kendell was already in her office when I arrived, looking every bit like the boyish detective I'd come to know over the last few weeks.

"Det. Kendall has explained that it was you who figured out Miss McDonald had killed Mrs. O'Brien."

I turned to Jace for verification on this.

"Since Ms. Windsor is now here," he started, "there is a little more to her story."

The D.A.'s eyes bounced between the two of us. "Which of you would care to share it with me then?"

Kendall made a face and scratched his head. "Ummm."

I pulled the pink glasses out of my purse. "These glasses belonged to the victim, Rose O'Brien. I purchased them at a thrift store a few weeks ago. When I put them on, I was transported if you will, into Rose's body... consciousness... I'm not sure how to explain it, but I was able to witness her murder, from her perspective. It is how I knew it was a female in red high heels who killed her. I saw the killer's shoes yesterday at the nursing home and realized it was Sarah McDonald who had killed Rose."

A flummoxed look crossed her face. She opened her mouth, closed her mouth, blinked several times and then set back in her chair; her hands flat upon her desk.

"What?" Her biting stare told me she was irritated with our, or my, explanation. "How in the hell, am I going to present that in a court of law?"

Neither Kendall or I moved or spoke a word.

"Kendall?" The D.A. barked after several moments of awkward silence.

He jumped like someone had hit him with a cattle prod and stammered, "I... I don't know. Everything Ms. Windsor relayed to me a few weeks ago, is exactly what transpired the day Rose O'Brien was killed, according to Sarah McDonald's confession."

I had to admit, it brought a sense of pleasure to me, seeing he was in the hot seat for once, at least until her next remark.

"What makes you think she's not involved," the prosecutor asked, nodding in my direction, "since she is familiar with all the details to the crime and crime scene?"

"Hey, I wasn't even in the state when Rose O'Brien was murdered," I snapped indignantly, suddenly finding my voice. "I have an iron clad alibi."

"I'm going to bet that Jack the Ripper did as well, hence the reason he was never caught," she gave me a pointed stare.

I wrinkled my brow at her and pointed at Kendall. "I've already taken enough abuse from him; I don't need to take it from you too.

"I could have thrown those damn glasses away when I found out what they showed, but no, I subjected myself to ridicule from the detective here and did my civic duty to help bring a killer to justice. So, I would appreciate not having accusations thrown my way or being compared to Jack the Ripper," I huffed.

Not only did I surprise myself with my emboldened speech and tirade, but I could also see the shock registered on Det. Kendall's face. If all else failed, I was going to blame the concussion and the medication the ER doctor had put me on, for the outburst.

Needless to say, the D.A. didn't feel my testimony would be believable, and she could only imagine the heyday the defense attorney would have with it.

Kendall caught up with me in the hallway after the D.A. had dismissed us.

"Remember all of those headaches Rita McDonald was having?" He asked.

"Yeah, what about them?" I asked in return.

"From what she told us in her statement, she suspected it might have been Sarah who had killed Rose. The stress and strain of the knowledge had caused her headaches to increase in strength and frequency. She just refused to believe that her daughter could have done something so heinous. But after Sarah's confession, she told us her suspicions."

"Is Rita going to be charged with anything?"

"I doubt it."

**

About four weeks after Sarah McDonald's arrest, I received a letter in the mail from Ethel.

Dear Marlie,

I hope you're doing well after Sarah hit you with that chair. I'm so sorry you had to go through all of this. I'm still in shock knowing it was Sarah. Her mother is quite devastated.

I had to beg Amelia's forgiveness for so many things. I carry so much guilt now knowing it was my granddaughter who killed Rose. She's not my biological granddaughter. Her mother married my son when she was three years old, though I've always loved her as if she were my own flesh and blood. I had no idea she harbored such resentment over me coming in 2nd place all these years.

I wanted to thank you for not listening to a foolish old woman and having sense enough to save the letter I asked you to throw away and give it back to Amelia. She brought it back to me and told me she had found it among Rose's things and was sure Rose would want me to have it. It's the last thing I have of my dearest friend. If you'd have listened to me, I wouldn't have this memento of our friendship. I will always be eternally grateful to you.

Nurse Cratchit told me you're not volunteering anymore, but if you are ever interested in visiting an old woman, I'd welcome you anytime. Don't take too long though, I've been reminded that it is myself and not Rose who has Alzheimer's and it seems to be getting worse day by day. I look forward to hearing from you.

Love, Ethel.

Ethel's letter brought a smile to my face. It was refreshing to see she had finally spoken to Amelia and accepted the last correspondence from Rose. It was also hysterical to me that she was still referring to Betty Stallworth as nurse Cratchit. She really did not care for the woman.

Once Rose's murder had been solved, Willow Glenn Senior Living had been inundated with volunteers, I suspect it gave some of the volunteers and employees something to talk about. I passed the baton to those younger and with more time on their hands. I'd certainly miss Ethel, my Navy captain, Mary from Kentucky and all those other delightful characters I'd come in contact with during my time at Willow Glenn.

**

A few days after Ethel's letter came, I took Rose's glasses back into the storeroom. I'd promised Helen that once the murder was solved, I would put them into our stock.

I put them on, one last time, expecting to find myself sitting in Rose's rocking chair with the knitting and the cats. To my surprise, when I peered through the lenses, the only thing visible was the inventory on the shelves. I guess solving the mystery had freed the images from within the rhinestone decorated frames. Either that or the second blow to my head had cured my paranormal affliction. I actually hoped it was both.

"Rest in peace, Rose," I eulogized solemnly, wrapping the glasses in tissue paper and putting them on a shelf.

An Interview with Det. Jace Kendall

Sitting in the chair across from me, is a well-dressed man, in his mid-thirties. Once he settles into place, I will begin our interview. He sits tall and erect, no slouch to his posture. His dark hair is offset by his intense blue eyes. I'd wager to say his steel blue eyed stare has elicited a confession or two during his time as a homicide detective.

Author: Today we are here with Det. Jace Kendall, of the Colorado Springs Police Department. Thank you for taking time out of your busy schedule to join us. I'm sure our readers would like to know your thoughts on what happened here. Tell me about the first time you met Ms. Windsor.

Author's note: I can see the hint of a smile as the detective begins to talk about meeting Ms. Windsor.

Kendall: Ms. Windsor is a unique individual. (*Here, I have the benefit of seeing the full smirk which Marlie so often complains about.*) When I pulled into the parking lot that morning, I noticed a woman sitting in her car. I assumed she was speaking to someone on the phone through a headset. After a while, I looked out the window of my office, about thirty minutes later, and saw she was still there. I went down to the parking lot to see if she might need some help. I'm sure I scared the crap out of her when I knocked on her window, because she jumped like a cat whose tail has been stepped on.

Author: What were your thoughts when you found out why she was there?

Kendall: I was surprised when she pulled out Rose O'Brien's glasses. I mean those glasses were pretty unique. After I had coaxed her into talking to me, it took everything I had not to laugh, when she blurted out her explanation for being there. I thought one of the other cops had put her up to it, as a gag.

But I grew a little suspicious after we were in my office and she started giving me details of the crime, because none of the officers working the case would have disclosed the information that she was giving me. We hadn't said anything about Mrs. O'Brien making tea for her friend, Ethel MacDonald, in the press release after the murder.

My gut told me she wasn't the killer, but she knew a lot of things she shouldn't. I did a background check on her after she left and couldn't find any connection to Mrs. O'Brien. But Ms. Windsor was on my radar.

And then the crazy broad turned up as a volunteer at the nursing home. She didn't have any past association with Willow Glenn, so I found it odd when I found her there.

Author: Why did you go back to Willow Glenn after your visit from Ms. Windsor?

Kendall: We had been pretty much focused on the maintenance guy, Frank Dennison. There had been some noise about him pilfering things from the residents. Since we thought it was a robbery gone wrong, it was where we had mistakenly concentrated our investigation. Then, he just disappeared. An APB went out and he surfaced in

Boca Raton, Florida. He was busted when he tried to pawn the stolen goods.

Even though all the evidence pointed to a burglary gone wrong in the O'Brien case, I would have been remiss in my duties if I hadn't at least considered an alternative scenario after speaking with Ms. Windsor.

Author: And what were your thoughts when she came to see you the second time?

Kendall: When she showed up the second time, I thought about calling the psych ward at Memorial. I was blown away when she mentioned one of the knitting needles was pulled from the body. It was something else we hadn't disclosed to the media. Ethel MacDonald, who found the body, made a statement which suggested that both knitting needles had been left in the body, so we kept the information about the one needle being removed, within the department.

I thought for a while, that perhaps, she had committed the murder and was trying to deflect blame to some phantom woman in red shoes, minimizing her role in the crime. After she left, I looked into her alibi for the time of the murder and found she had indeed been in Nashville visiting her sister. But I just couldn't bring myself to believe this supernatural stuff she was trying to sell me.

Author: And now?

The detective doesn't answer this question right away. I could tell he was thinking about his response.

Kendall: I'm still not sure I believe in the supernatural. But everything Ms. Windsor told me, fleshed out. So...who's to say?

The detective gives me an unconvincing shrug.

Author: Were you shocked when she called you to tell you she'd found the murderer?

Kendall: Yes, I was. I became extremely concerned when the line went dead while I was speaking with her. I grabbed a couple of uniforms and rushed up to the north side. We fanned out when we got there. There were voices coming from down a hallway. It was then I overheard Sarah MacDonald telling her grandmother how she had killed Mrs. O'Brien because of the contest, and I discovered Ms. Windsor bound in transparent tape on the floor. It hadn't occurred to me the knitting contest would be a possible motive.

Ethel MacDonald had seen her granddaughter heading down the hallway and thought maybe something had happened to Sarah's mother, Rita, so she'd followed her. I can't imagine the shock the poor woman felt when she heard her granddaughter's confession.

Author: So, would you be more inclined to believe Ms. Windsor if she came to you again with something like this in the future?

Kendall: I'm not sure. I'm just hoping this was a one-time thing. We can't have civilians get caught up in investigations. Ms. Windsor was fortunate she wasn't killed. If this paranormal stuff is real, it's creepy as hell and I'm not sure I want to head down that road.

Author: I'm sure our readers have more questions, but I know you're busy and have a prior engagement. So, I'd like to thank-you for your time this morning and candid responses.

Kendall: My pleasure.

This time it isn't his infamous smirk that crosses his lips, but a genuine smile. He stands to leave, his 6'1" frame looming over me. His handshake is firm but gentle as he wishes me a good day and quietly exits my office.

Oh Death, Where's Thy Sting

A Secondhand Homicide Whodunit (Book 2)

1

Today was shopping day, it was time to restock the inventory for The Back Porch on Bijou. Not that our shelves were bare, but you always needed to be on the lookout for anything special and unique. I had wandered up and down each and every isle, spending almost an hour inside Open Hands Christian Goods, placing a few items into my shopping cart here and there. That was, until a cute little, floppy, gardening hat captured my attention.

Even though I live in a monstrosity of an apartment complex, I still enjoy growing flowers and an occasional tomato plant or two on my second story balcony. Locating a mirror, I tried the hat on… huge mistake!

"Oh, hell no!" I groaned, swiping the floppy hat from my head, and tossing it back onto the pile of accessories. Dread loomed within me and anxiety crept into my body, tremors dancing their way down my fingers. *Not this again*, I sighed inwardly my stomach settling somewhere near my toes.

Several other patrons glanced my direction at my vocalized outburst, looking me up and down as if I had just committed a mortal sin or something. All I said was 'hell', I mean, there was a long list of other colorful expletives I could have used instead. Sheesh.

About six months ago, I'd had a skiing accident, which had changed my life, and not for the better, let me assure you. Ok, so I really fell on the ice and cracked my skull, but skiing accident sounds so much more interesting, don't you think? Anyway, since that bump to my head, I had seen the murder of a woman, while looking through the glasses she was wearing when she died. The glasses had been donated to charity after her death and I just happened to be the one to buy them.

I co-own a small, vintage boutique in Colorado Springs, so I spend a good amount of time in these secondhand shops, looking for the perfect items for my own store and my clients.

When I'd placed the floppy canvas hat upon my head, I had suddenly found myself on my knees, in front of an enormous flower bed, filled with an array of colors and scents. I was *not* ready to go back on that gruesome game show. I'll take murder for $200, Alex. No way, Jose.

After staring at the hat for what seemed like an eternity, I cautiously picked it back up, turning it over in my hands. I reasoned that maybe he wasn't murdered, maybe he died of natural causes with his hat on. Images of the wild west flashed through my mind, as I envisioned cowboys in gunfights, dying with their boots on. My mind works like that sometimes. Dying with their boots on, dying with their hat on, seemed like a logical connection to me.

And besides, why would a murder victim's hat be in a Christian thrift shop? Doing the un-sensible thing, I bought the hat and prayed for the best. If this person really was a murder victim… I needed to be sure.

Securing my purchases, I made my way to the parking lot and climbed into the Jeep. The cashier had put the hat into the bottom of one of the bags. So, after dumping the contents onto the passenger seat, I scooped up the gardening hat and plopped it atop my head for the second time within thirty minutes.

Once again, I found myself kneeling in front of a neatly manicured flower bed. Leaning in, I breathed in the heady floral scents. Sweet smelling blooms of pink dianthus, intermixed with white roses and peonies, tickled my olfactory nerves. A man's gloved hands reached forward and pulled out three or four yellow dandelions and several strands of roving bindweed, with its delicate white blossoms; then tossed them onto a pile of discarded weeds. I scooched over a few feet, leaned, and breathed in the heavenly scents of a different bunch of flowers, repeating the weeding process in this new section of the garden. Weeding was yielding a therapeutic quality to the man's gardening experience; I could feel his inner peace.

My eyes were drawn to a straw-colored bump sitting amongst the rainbow of blossoming posies. Confusion clouded my consciousness. *That's odd, who would put a bee skep in the middle of my garden? Those aren't even used anymore, and everyone knows that I'm allergic to bees.* These thoughts seeped into my mind, a man's voice uttering the concern. His gloved hand reached for the skep, lingering momentarily. Upon lifting it, several dozen bees poured out from underneath the small woven hive with an angry droning din.

I could feel panic rise in the man's chest, as the bees buzzed around his head. He clenched his teeth. The muscles in his neck tensed in terror and his hands began to tremble. Swallowing his fear, he gently tried waving them away as he struggled to back up on his knees. Ouch! Shaking his hand in pain, he pulled off a large, leather work glove. A hot, red spot was visible on the back of his right hand. Burning pain spread down his fingers and his hand throbbed with each beat of his heart. Waving the buzzing cluster of bees away from his face, only seemed to

193

agitate the tiny creatures. He began swatting wildly at the buzzing insects swarming about him.

I heard a gentle tap, tap, tap before the bam, bam, bam. I ripped the hat off, my head swiveling wildly about. A woman with graying hair was frantically pounding on my driver's side window and shouting at me. I turned the key one click and rolled down the electric glass barrier.

"Are you all right? You looked like you might be having a seizure. Should I call 911?" A nervousness was reflected in her wavering voice.

Turning my head slowly, and scanning the parking lot, I realized I had drawn quite a crowd. People of all ages gawked at me from all four sides of my vehicle, peering in through my tinted windows. I could hear a general mumbling undulating through the assembled mass.

I looked back at the woman, my mouth agape.

"There's a bee in my car. I don't like bees," I said, scrunching up my face and shaking my head.

"Oh, sweetie," the elderly woman said in a soft southern accent, as she waved a hand in my direction, "a little ol' bee ain't gonna to hurt you none."

Tell that to my murder victim, I thought, forcing a smile to my lips.

"Thank-you for the concern," I started my car and rolled all four windows down. "I hope it flies out while I'm driving."

The woman with the southern accent announced to the throng surrounding my car, "She was afraid of a little ol' bee, that's all."

With my car in drive, I pulled away from my audience. I certainly wasn't going to win an Oscar with that pathetic performance. My disapproving public showed their disdain with the rolling of eyes and shaking of heads, visible in my rearview mirror. Thus, ending my short and not so sweet acting career.

At the stoplight, I rolled up my windows. Truly, I am not afraid of bees. I had once tried to talk the apartment manager into letting me keep a small hive at the edge of the property a while back, but I was told that under no certain circumstances would that be possible. He gave me some mumbo jumbo about city ordinances. Oh well, maybe someday I'd have the funds to buy up a plot of land to build a comfortable home, raise bees and grow a *real* garden. Maybe I'd have a couple of chickens too. And a goat.

I needed to find a place to finish this new vision, someplace where I could have a moment to myself, without interruption and away from prying eyes. Scanning both sides of the street as I drove down Academy, I pulled into a car wash, at some random gas station. Once inside and with the wash started, I put the hat back on.

About the Author

Myrl V. Williams is a Colorado native and devoted mother, daughter, sister, and aunt. Like Marlie, Myrl lives in Colorado Springs with her adorable shih tzu, Laeto. Inspiration for Marlie's crazy exploits comes from family/friend stories and a file she keeps called 'Stuff My Sister Says' though the real title is slightly more colorful.

Her works include the Secondhand Homicide Whodunit series featuring Marlie Windsor, the If These Walls Could Talk series and an array of short stories.

The Secondhand Homicide Whodunit series developed after seeing a writing prompt on social media, she tweaked it to incorporate the cozy mystery vibe she felt upon seeing the prompt. As she began establishing the characters and setting, the entire story line erupted like 'Old Faithful'.

Email her at: authormyrlvwilliams@gmail.com
Facebook: https://www.facebook.com/MyrlVWilliams